I0546593

His Beautiful Bea

A Touches of Austen Novella

LEENIE BROWN

Leenie B Books

Halifax

Dear Reader,

THIS NOVELLA IS THE beginning of my Touches of Austen series. The stories in this series feature original characters and plots that have been touched in some way by the influence of Jane Austen and her novels. The story you hold in your hand, *His Beautiful Bea*, has elements in it that harken back to *Mansfield Park* (one of this author's favourite Austen novels).

To help you on your way to seeing the influence of Jane Austen's writing on this novella, I will tell you two of the items that pay homage to the original work.

First, we have Beatrice Tierney, who shares some similarities in character to Fanny Price. She is quiet and shrinks from notice, but perhaps not to the extent that Fanny does because, unlike Fanny, Bea lives with her mother and brother, both of whom she loves dearly. Having this loving foundation has helped the naturally reserved Beatrice to be less anxious.

Secondly, there is Stratsbury Park and its residents. Stratsbury is owned by Sir Herbert Clayton, who has two sons — the elder, Graeme is a rather free-spirited sort of gentleman, while his younger brother, Everett, is on the more reserved side. These two brothers are based in part on the Bertram brothers. Beatrice is, of course, infatuated with the younger Clayton son. However, this is not *Mansfield Park*, and I have chosen to arrange the romantic results differently.

There are other nods to Austen in this story. Some were purposefully done, others just serendipitously happened. Which ones will you notice?

Happy Reading!

Chapter 1

GRAEME CLAYTON'S PRETTY NEIGHBOUR, Beatrice Tierney, blew out a breath, settled back against a tree in Stratsbury Park's garden, and attempted to find a comfortable position in which to read. Graeme pushed off the garden wall, against which he had been leaning as he watched Bea, and walked in her direction

The weather was warm, but not unbearably so, and the shade cast by the sprawling canopy of leaves above Bea surely provided a pleasant respite from the rays of the sun. That was good. Bea did not do well when she became overly warm. Hers was not the strongest constitution. Illness seemed to like her just as much as everyone else did.

A blessed, cooling breeze occasionally fluttered the hem of her skirt and attempted to turn the pages of her book. Graeme could just imagine how that would begin to annoy

Bea soon enough. She did not like to have her reading interrupted by anyone or anything. Of course, it was not the breeze that was going to put a stop to her reading.

She darted a glance in the direction of her cousins, Felicity and Grace Love. Her lips twitched with displeasure as she turned her attention back to her book. It was an interesting expression, but not unexpected since the elder Miss Love, Miss Felicity Love, had claimed the attention of Graeme's younger brother, Everett.

From the time Bea had met Everett, she had followed him around with a particular look on her face that spoke of her adoration. It was not an obvious expression. It was simply an unmistakable softness in her eyes and the tipping up ever so slightly of the corners of her mouth.

Bea brushed away a fly that was meandering a path across the words she was attempting to decipher just as Graeme cast a long shadow across the page, causing her to look up to see its source.

"Is it a difficult passage?" Graeme chuckled as her lips puckered into a deeper scowl.

He knew very well that Bea was not short on intelligence. She might be quiet, verging on the edge of overly reserved and gentle, but it was not due to lack of intellect. In fact, when she did open her mouth to speak on any subject, her comments were impressively well-thought-out. He knew that she studied things — mulling them over and over, assessing them from every possible angle, and then, and only then, having decided she had a good grasp of her ideas, her thoughts on a matter might be shared. Equally as often as not, however, she would merely smile softly, raise a brow, and remain silent. It perplexed him how she could keep her opinions to herself so often. He had a devil of a time keeping his tongue from saying exactly what was in his head.

She was not the only one of the two of them who observed things to assess the lie of the land. Graeme was an expert in observation himself. For instance, today, for the past twenty minutes, he had been watching Bea. She had sighed and shaken her head often, her lips had pursed, her brow had furrowed, and the pages of her book had not flipped in all that time. She was contemplating something, and he was rather certain he knew what it was.

He took a seat next to her on the ground and, giving her shoulder a nudge with his, repeated his question, earning him a very pretty scowl. However, as quickly as the scowl had formed on her lips, it melted away into the pleasant expression she wore in company when she would rather be elsewhere but did not wish to offend.

She was about to deny there was any issue at all — much as she always did. Others were permitted to be displeased and out of sorts, but Bea never allowed herself to be so — at least, not in company. One had to look for more subtle clues as to how Bea was really feeling, but that was just one of the things that made her uniquely his Bea.

"No," she began her denial, just as he had predicted she would, "the passage is not difficult. I was just distracted by the excellent weather."

Graeme, who was not content to let the situation pass so neatly, snatched her book out of her hands. It might be entirely possible to provoke her into revealing the truth of what he suspected.

"Your distraction has nothing to do with my brother?" he asked as he snapped the book closed on her marker.

Ah, there was her look of panic — a slight widening of the eyes and a sharp, though quiet, inhale of breath. He had obviously hit on the very thing which she was valiantly attempting to conceal.

Though they were only neighbours, Bea and her brother, Maxwell, had spent so many hours in company with Graeme and Everett that Graeme felt he knew the Tierney siblings almost as well as he knew his own brother. Well, "only neighbours" was perhaps not the most accurate way to describe who the Tierneys were to the Claytons.

Captain Tierney and Sir Herbert Clayton had been friends since childhood, and when the captain had come into some money — enough to buy a small estate for his family — he had settled on Heathcote which was not more than four miles distance from the western boundary of Stratsbury Park. And in such a manner had begun a closer friendship between their families. They had spent many days and evenings in one another's company during that first month after the Tierneys' arrival at Heathcote.

And then had come the day when Captain Tierney had been required to return to his ship. He had called on his friend Sir Herbert the evening before his departure and extracted a promise to care for Mrs. Tierney and his children if something unfortunate should befall him. As fate would have it, the unfortunate did befall the captain, and he had never returned from sea.

Bea had borne the news with far more fortitude than Graeme had expected to find in one so young and female. It was then that he had taken a greater liking to her. She was not like the silly girls he had met over the years. She was unique in her quiet strength and resolve and so very unlike himself that he found himself compelled to attempt an understanding of such a person. His reward had been a comfortable friendship that allowed him access to the Beatrice others looking on would likely not suspect existed.

He nudged her shoulder again. "I do not believe it was the weather disturbing your reading," he whispered. "Are you positive your distraction has nothing to do with my brother?"

Bea shrugged.

Seeing he was not likely to get more of a reply from Bea than that, Graeme switched tactics and pressed on. "Miss Love is very pretty. How old is she now?"

Bea heaved a sigh. "Felicity is nineteen, just as I am, and Grace is seventeen."

"Are they both out?" he asked, moving her book away from the hand that attempted to reclaim it. He was not leaving this spot today without finding out if his suspicions about Bea's feelings for his brother were correct.

"Yes," Bea's lips stretched into a thin smile. "I have been regaled with the delights of the season several times since their arrival a fortnight ago."

Graeme shifted, placing the book on the grass next to him and stretching out his legs.

"Will you be going to town this next season? I could make a good number of introductions for you, and even with your modest dowry, I believe, we could find you a suitable husband."

He had not even finished speaking before her head was shaking back and forth.

"You will not go? I thought Max said he had put aside enough to give you a bit of a season."

"I do not wish to go. I have no desire to endure the crushes about which my cousins have told me. I prefer our small assemblies here."

"I imagine it will be harder to find a gentleman worthy of you here, but I have not been to an assembly in some time. Perhaps there is someone who has already captured your heart?" He tipped his head and studied her face carefully, looking for any indication that there might be a gentleman she already preferred.

The signs he sought were there — the slight blush on her cheek and the lowering of her eyes — but he chose to ignore them and continued on.

"There is always Bath. I would assume the crowds there are not so great as they are in London, and Mother has been forever begging father to take her there. I am certain she would enjoy taking you along. She does enjoy your company."

Bea ran a finger absent-mindedly along the chain that held a pendant Graeme knew contained a lock of her father's hair. Between that action and the way in which she had pulled the corner of her bottom lip between her teeth, he knew she was considering the possibility of going to Bath. However, as fascinating as that fact was, it did not help him discern her feelings about his brother. So, he circled around to Everett once again.

"Everett is planning one last go of the season before he takes up his position."

Bea nodded. "I know."

There was an interesting sadness to her tone.

"Unless, of course, he finds a lady before then. Perhaps Miss Love will be capable of finally snaring him."

There it was — a small, sad, fleeting frown. It was true. Beatrice Tierney was in love with his brother — the fortunate clod. Hailed as the more studious of the two Clayton brothers, what Everett possessed in the ability to apply himself to his studies and excel, he lacked in his capacity to see the subtly obvious before him. However, Graeme would contemplate how his brother could have missed recognizing Bea's preference for him later. Right now, he needed to make Bea smile.

"Many have tried to bring him up to scratch, you know, but none have succeeded. He is a handsome devil — much like his older brother."

Bea chuckled. "He is, at least, humbler than his brother," she chided.

"So, you do not deny that the Clayton brothers are handsome?" Graeme teased.

Bea rolled her eyes. "I am not blind," she said with a light swat to Graeme's arm.

"Neither am I," Graeme retorted.

Bea's brow furrowed in confusion.

"I am not speaking of being blind to my own comeliness." He smiled at her. "For I assure you that I know precisely how fetching I look." He winked and then chuckled as she once again rolled her eyes. It was always a joy to provoke her just enough to elicit a small response such as he had just received.

"I see many things clearly. For instance, I can see that Miss Love and Miss Grace are attractive and well-skilled in all the arts required to capture a husband." He shrugged. "There are many such ladies in London, who, if they wish for a desired outcome, will do their best to achieve it no matter the ploys and scheming necessary."

He nodded in response to her wide-eyed questioning look. "A fellow has to tread carefully. However, that is not all I see clearly."

"It is not?"

"No, it is not." He crossed his arms and leaned against the trunk of the tree with his shoulder resting lightly against hers and his arm wishing to wrap around her and pull her close to his side as he had done when she was just a girl. However, she was no longer a mere child, and he was not her brother, so unless he wished to get scolded and have her dash away, neither of which would assist his cause, he refrained.

"I also see the way you look at my brother, and frankly, he is a fool to ignore you. I would not ignore a lady of beauty and good character such as yourself if she was to look at me so longingly." He pressed his lips together to keep from chuckling at the quick breath she drew. He had shocked her just as he had planned.

"I do no such thing," Bea refuted weakly.

"Lying does not become you, my beautiful Bea."

"Do not call me that. I am not beautiful."

He peeked over at her. Her cheeks were aflame as he knew they would be.

"My dear, if there is one thing I know, it is beautiful women, and you are definitely beautiful – beguiling, even, when you blush so prettily." He reached out a hand and grabbed her arm to prevent her from jumping to her feet and running away. Bea did not like compliments of her person or actions. She preferred to fade into the background — to act without recognition or praise, qualities that would serve a parson's wife well, but also qualities that made it easy for a numbskull, soon-to-be parson, like his brother to overlook her.

"Now," he said, holding her arm firmly as she tried to pull it out of his grasp, "as I have said, I am of the belief that my brother is an idiot and Miss Love is a grasping...," he cleared his throat, "something that is not appropriate for a lady's ears."

Bea's eyes grew wide, and her head tilted as she looked out toward where Felicity was talking in a very animated fashion to her sister while clinging to Everett's arm.

"I saw both her and her sister in London," Graeme whispered near Bea's ear.

"Then, why did you ask me if they were both out?" She gasped as his lips brushed her cheek when she turned her head.

He smirked and shrugged. "I am a cad and wished to hear your opinion of them."

"Which I did not give," she pulled on her arm again, finally freeing it from his hold.

"Oh, but you did," he replied. "Your tone and the shortness of your replies told me all I need to know. You are not pleased with them — or more precisely, you are not pleased with Miss Love since she is the one who has enchanted my brother."

"I have never enjoyed my cousins," Bea refuted. "We have little in common. They like fashion and soirees while I prefer books and domestic pursuits. However, you have never been home when they visited before so you would not know how very unalike we are."

He chuckled. "Deny it if you must, but you are jealous." He climbed to his feet and extended a hand to her.

Bea looked at his hand warily.

"Come. You cannot sit here the full day. Mother will wish to know you took some exercise. She worries about you."

Bea's brow furrowed as she studied his face. "You will not say shocking things, and your lips will not touch me?"

A hint of mischief touched his smile. "You know I am constitutionally incapable of not saying something shocking at some point, but I shall refrain from touching any part of you other than your fingers with my lips."

Bea sighed and shook her head, but a touch of amusement curled her lips into a small smile as she placed her hand in his and allowed him to help her to her feet.

"Good heavens," he muttered as he pulled her upright, "if my brother does not marry you, I might. When you smile like that, it is difficult not to wish to break my promise to confine my lips to just your fingers."

He winked as her mouth dropped open. "As I said, I am constitutionally incapable of not being shocking." He tucked her hand into the crook of his arm.

He was teasing her, of course — at least, partially. She was both beautiful and beguiling, but if she were not so obviously lovesick for his brother and if she were not Bea, his friend and the closest thing he had to a sister; he would be hard-pressed not to consider her as the next Lady Clayton.

Chapter 2

LAUGHTER AND WHISPERS WAFTED on the breeze that blew through the open garden doors at the far right hand side of the blue drawing room at Stratsbury Park later that day. Grace and Felicity were gathered with Everett and Graeme near the piano at the opposite end of the room.

Beatrice began, once again, to read the page of the book which lay open before her. How many times had she tried to read this same page while sitting in the garden? She should likely turn back a few pages and begin reading there, for though the words from the pages had passed through her mind, not one of them had made an impression.

If only Felicity were not such a flirt, and if only Everett had ever seen Bea as more than his friend's little sister, then, maybe, this day would not be the drudgery it was turning out to be. Maybe then, she would be able to read without distraction. It was not as if she was only capable of reading in a silent room. She was proficient at reading in the sitting room at Heathcote while her brother and mother had a discussion. However, the idea that Everett was so taken with her cousin had rendered her powerless against distraction or worse, victim to it.

"You are a fair sight to see," Max Tierney said as he plopped down next to her and flicked her book. "I am surprised you have not finished this yet. I half expected you to be ready to peruse the library for another to replace it before we leave today, but you have more than half of this book left to read."

Bea smiled at her brother. He was not a great reader. He preferred being out of doors and being busy to sitting and reading. However, he was the dearest and best brother for whom a lady could wish, and he found her love of reading to be something about which to be proud. She had heard stories from her mother and Lady Clayton about how challenging it was for some book-loving ladies to find husbands. Apparently, whether it was true or not, according to Lady Clayton and her mother, social convention promoted ladies who preferred more sociable pursuits. Thankfully, Max was not one of those sorts of gentlemen, and there was hope that whomever her sister-in-law ended up being, she would be a lady with more than feathers for brains.

"I promise I shall not disappoint you," she replied. "I have completed my book of poetry and would like to replace it, and Sir Herbert has already promised me that I can borrow another from his library. Will you help me choose a new book?" She knew his answer before he said it. The library at Stratsbury Park was not so dear to him as it was to her.

Max shook his head and laughed. "Not likely. My knowledge of poetry is limited."

Of course, he would assist her if she truly needed him to, but she knew that he knew she did not require help finding something to read. The most help she might require would be reaching a shelf.

He stretched out his arms, resting them on the back of the sofa with one wrapped around her shoulders. "I know a few poets and poems, but not a vast array. You would do better to ask Everett or even Graeme. They would know more."

Even in his refusal he was offering his help. She could not fault him for his care of her at present. "Then, if I require assistance, my dear brother, I will ask one of them and not you."

"I will be eternally grateful."

She laughed softly as Max squeezed her shoulder. "Did you enjoy your walk?" she asked.

Everett and Max, accompanied by Felicity and Grace, had left the garden at one point, and had meandered down some path in the wilderness. Graeme had suggested that he and she follow, but Bea, who, due to the lingering effects of a childhood fever, tired more easily than most ladies, had thought it best to return to the house since there was a full afternoon of entertainment and dinner yet to come.

Graeme had not been disappointed and readily acquiesced, admitting that he preferred not to hear the babblings of flighty females in his own garden. Apparently, listening to such ladies in London was acceptable if one was at a ball or some other function. However, in the privacy of one's own estate, such activities should be avoided as much as was possible. Yet, despite his objections to such things, he would have suffered them for her sake. For all his taunting and teasing, he was very caring. She was blessed to have been left in the care of such good men by her father. Of course, neither Graeme nor Max had been men when her father had died.

"I wish you had joined us." Max rubbed her shoulder as he often did when he wished to soothe her. Apparently, he knew that she was not pleased to have been left behind.

"You did not seem inconvenienced by my absence. In fact, you did not even bother to ask me to join you." She pursed her lips, and her brows furrowed. Max was one of the few people to whom she ever spoke so freely. "I am surprised you even remembered I was here."

Max tugged her closer and kissed her head. "Oh, come now, Bea. You were pleased to sit and read. Do not tell me you would rather have listened to our cousins regale you with stories of their adventures in town."

She shrugged. It was not the fact that she had been left to return to the house that bothered her, as that was her preference. It was the feeling of being utterly forgotten – that is, she had felt forgotten by everyone but Graeme.

"Still struggling with that passage, I see." The very gentleman about whom she had been thinking perched himself on the arm of the sofa. He nudged her leg with his. "Slide over so I can sit properly before Mother lectures."

Bea peered up at him. Graeme was another person to whom she felt comfortable being less than accommodating and often spoke as freely with him as she did with her brother. "There is room beside Max."

"I do not wish to sit next to Max and have his arm draped around me. Slide over." He batted his lashes. "Please." He chuckled when she made a small, exasperated sound.

Oh! He was trying. Why he found it so enjoyable to provoke her beyond the bounds of propriety at times was beyond her. It was nearly, but not quite so, exasperating as her delight in his taunting. However, she knew that he was the sort of gentleman who was playful with his friends, and she liked being counted as his friend. It was likely that in which her delight was founded.

"Very well." She nudged Max, who moved over, pulling her with him as Graeme slid down the curved arm and into the corner of the sofa.

"She needs a new book of poetry," Max said, leaning around Bea to talk to Graeme. "I have told her to see you or Everett if she needs help choosing one."

Graeme once again snatched Bea's book from her. "She has not even finished this one. Why ever would she need another?"

"My book, if you would," Bea said, holding out her hand. "And that is a novel, not poetry."

Graeme smiled, and with a small shake of his head, tucked the book between his leg and the arm of the sofa. "Reading is for when you are alone." He tilted his head and looked at her with a teasing glint in his eye. "Unless, of course, you would like me to read to you."

"Are you courting my sister?" Max asked with a laugh.

Between his kissing her cheek earlier – which Max did not and would not ever know about – and Graeme's offer to read to her now, the question seemed a good one, except for one particularly important thing. This was Graeme. Graeme was nearly a brother to her. A handsome, completely-not-related-to her brother. She studied his profile. It was not all sharp edges, but it was not soft curves either. There was a definite manliness to it that she was certain helped him charm ladies in town. The way he often refused to be clean shaven, preferring to have a bit of a shadow of a beard was quite becoming. Perhaps, she decided on such an examination, dear friend would be a better classification for Graeme than nearly a brother was.

After all, a lady could find a brother handsome. However, finding him somewhat desirable was wrong, and Bea could not deny that she was comfortable admitting that Graeme Clayton was desirable.

"Gentlemen can read to ladies without courting them," Graeme retorted. "Have you never read to your sister?"

"I prefer to read to myself," Bea replied before her brother could.

Max read to both her and their mother at times, just as her father had done. It was a lovely tradition, but when she wished to thoroughly enjoy a book by rereading and pausing to ponder things, such as now, she would rather do the reading herself.

"If you would kindly return my book, Mr. Clayton."

Graeme ignored her request, for, as it turned out, he had come with one of his own.

"Miss Grace has proposed playing whist. They will need a fourth to complete their set."

"I thought they were going to play the piano," Bea said in some confusion. Was that not why Felicity was sorting through music and batting her lashes at Everett? Her cousins certainly did flit easily from one thing to another!

"No, there shall be singing and playing after dinner. They are only selecting their pieces now," Graeme explained. "So, do you wish to be their fourth? I said I would ask."

"They would far rather have Max," Bea assured him.

"No, I asked Everett which Tierney he would like me to ask to join them, and he specifically asked me to inquire of you, not Max."

"Oh," was the only reply Bea gave for a moment. The idea that Everett should request her was rather pleasant even though she knew it was her ability to pay attention to the game better than her brother did which recommended her. No matter the reason, he had preferred her, and she would be happy with that. It was a step in the right direction after all. "I suppose I could endure one round."

"I thought you might," Graeme whispered with a wink.

She shook her head and pleaded with her eyes that he would not say anything more. It was bad enough that he had managed to extract a confession about her admiration of Everett from her earlier. She did not need her brother knowing that secret, too.

"Please, allow me to escort you to your table, my lady," Graeme said as he stood and extended his hand with a flourish.

Relief washed over her. He would keep her secret. She should have known he would. He had always been trustworthy. Some lady, someday, was going to be truly fortunate to have him for her husband. Of course, that day was likely a long way off, for Graeme was, by his own admission, in no hurry to leave being a bachelor behind.

Chapter 3

"MISS ABERNATHY'S PLAYING WAS such a delight." Grace placed her card on the table.

For the pitiful little attention that the young woman was paying to her cards, she was playing as if she knew what she was doing. Surprisingly.

"But then the harp is so beautiful when played well," she continued as play passed to the next player. "Do you not think so, Beatrice?"

"I imagine it is. However, I have not had the pleasure of hearing a harp. Sadly, there are none of my acquaintances who play it."

How did she keep the tone of her voice sounding as if she were genuinely interested in what Miss Grace had to say?

Grace clucked her tongue. "Such a pity," she murmured.

According to Graeme, the pity was the way Miss Grace could talk about any subject for an extraordinarily long period of time. Miss Love had only to mention a topic and her sister was sure to have some story about it. For the most part, it seemed that Miss Grace was simply a chatterbox until she ended the discourse with a question about it to direct to either Everett or Bea.

"Perhaps," Bea agreed. "But then, I guess I will only ever be able to say how great a pity it is once I have heard a harp played as skillfully as you have described it."

Ah! There was his clever and not-altogether-pleased Bea. Graeme glanced around the group. No one, except perhaps for Max, appeared to know that Bea was being anything more than utterly kind. Not that Bea was being unkind, per se. It was just that her frustration with her cousins was beginning to fray her equanimity.

"And what about you, Mr. Everett Clayton, what do you think of the harp?" Grace asked.

And just like that, the attention shifted back to his brother.

Everett studied his cards, clearly oblivious to the ploys going on beside and across from him by the sisters Love. "I have always found the song of a harp to be a most ethereal one." He lay his selection and took the trick. "That is six for Miss Love and me," he said with a smile for Felicity, who sat opposite him. "Four more and we win."

"We are a very winning pair, are we not?" Felicity dipped her head and smiled as she asked it.

"Indeed, we are," Everett replied, his smile growing slightly.

Oblivious to the ploys did not mean he was unaffected by them. The blundering sap.

"I have not had this much success at whist since the last time that your cousin and I played our brothers at Christmas. Do you remember that?" Everett turned to his right and directed the question to Bea.

"I do. We were delightfully successful, much to our brothers' disappointment."

Bea's sweet smile and happy expression were lost on Graeme's unobservant brother because he had turned his eyes back to his cards after a quick return of Bea's smile. It was unlike him to be so inattentive. Graeme had seen many a lovesick swain become so in the presence of the lady whom they favoured, but he had honestly never expected it from his normally stalwart, rule-abiding brother.

"I think Bea and I could take the lot of you," Graeme grumbled. He was sitting just behind Bea and to her left, between her and his brother, and he was not at all pleased with the progression of the game at present. And it had nothing to do with who was winning or losing.

Bea was supposed to have partnered with Everett. That was the plan. However, before Graeme could convince Bea to take a spot at the table, Miss Love had weaseled her way into being Everett's partner. And for the entirety of the game thus far, the comments had been about this gown or that carriage, as well as several soirees that were absolutely the thing! She had directed the conversation to nothing that was of interest to either he or Bea, and from the look on Max's face, he was equally as disinterested in the Miss Loves' social calendar. It was enough to make Graeme's head spin and his blood simmer since it appeared that each story was specifically designed to show Bea at a disadvantage.

"Oh, then we shall deal you in at the next hand. I am certain my sister would not mind surrendering her seat to you for one round, would you dear?" Felicity turned to her sister with what Graeme classified as the most patronizing of smiles.

Grace blinked and looked first at Graeme and then her sister. There was definitely more innocence to Miss Grace than there was to her sister, for Graeme, who had made it a bit of a sport for himself to observe chits in the ballroom for their small unspoken conversations, did not miss the slight tip of Felicity's head toward Bea and her pleading eyes that flicked in Everett's direction.

Apparently, though Grace had yet to discern it, Felicity found Bea to be something of a threat. This was good,

Graeme supposed. It likely meant his brother had spoken about Bea and had not forgotten her completely when faced with the fawning and flirtatious Felicity.

"Most happily," Grace replied with a smile that was given a moment too late to be genuine.

"Very good then," Graeme said, settling back and crossing his arms, "pay attention to what is being played, and do not leave me in a place where it will be impossible to make ten before my brother does." Graeme ignored the scowl Everett gave him, as well as the flustered gasping noise Grace made.

"Mr. Clayton does not like to lose," Bea said.

She was, of course, trying to cover his rudeness, for she was a peacemaker at heart. Ruffled feathers were things she could not abide without some attempt to smooth them.

"He is rather intense when he plays," Bea continued. "It was not at all a pleasant evening when Mr. Everett Clayton and I beat Mr. Clayton and my brother."

"I should say it was not," muttered Max, who was sitting diagonally across the table from Graeme and between the two Miss Loves. "Graeme can be rather blustery when he is in a foul mood."

"And are you as blustery as he?" Grace lay a hand on Max's sleeve.

"Mind your cards," Graeme growled.

"None is so blustery as Mr. Clayton," Bea answered, turning to give Graeme a small teasing smile that caused him to catch his breath and swallow, instead of retorting.

Good heavens, his brother was a fool!

"I, on the other hand, do not care if we win or lose," Bea continued, "as either way my book shall be returned when our game has concluded." She pressed her lovely lips together. Likely to keep from looking even the smallest bit triumphant about reclaiming her beloved book.

Graeme raised his left eyebrow. "She jests. Bea enjoys winning just as much as I do. It is just that she is incapable of being anything less than gracious."

Idiot! he shouted in his mind while glaring at his brother. He doubted Miss Love contained two ounces of the good-natured temperament Bea possessed.

"You speak of my cousin very familiarly." Felicity gave Graeme a look that questioned his true relationship with Bea – or perhaps she was just hoping to push Bea in his direction and away from Everett.

Whatever her purpose in questioning his use of Bea's name was, it was not going to sway him from his goal. He would be dead and in his grave before he let a chit like Miss Felicity Love outwit him.

"My brother likes to flout social conventions when he can," Everett replied, once again laying his card, and taking the trick.

"I see no need for such formality with good friends of long-standing." Graeme stretched out his legs and purposefully bumped his brother – the idiot's – leg with his foot. "How old were you when you arrived at Heathcote, Bea?"

"Can you not figure that out yourself?" Max asked with a chuckle. "I would think you could since you know how old you were then, how old you are now, and how old my sister is. It is not a complicated calculation."

Graeme shrugged. "I prefer to allow Bea to save me the bother of such things." And he wished to give Bea an opportunity to speak about something of substance while highlighting the previous claim she held on both his and his brother's attentions and affections. It was likely that Everett would miss the point of the lesson since he was once again smiling at Felicity, but perhaps that lady would feel a small jab of something. Graeme did not care what the discomfort was named so long as Miss Love felt it. She had given enough of her own pokes and taunts over the course of the game.

"I was nine, Max was fifteen, as was your brother — no, that is not correct. Mr. Everett Clayton had just turned sixteen, and you were..."

Bea's lips curled into a small smile, and she tapped her lip with a finger as if she actually had to strain to remember his age.

The bumbling blockhead! Graeme's foot bumped his brother's once again as Graeme uncrossed and re-crossed his ankles. If Everett would pause for even one moment and take his eyes off his cards or Miss Love and looked — really looked — at Bea and the way her lips pursed into a perfectly kissable pucker before she decided she had calculated Graeme's age appropriately, there would be no way Everett could continue entertaining Miss Love when such a beguiling creature as Bea sat beside him.

"I believe, Mr. Clayton was an extremely ancient seventeen, were you not? Your birthday is in May, and we had arrived in March, just at the end."

"There is no fault with your memory," Graeme replied. "But do mind your cards."

"She only had to take her mind off them because you could not subtract ten from nineteen," protested Max, who was once again laughing at Graeme, not that it bothered Graeme in the least. He preferred not to be taken too seriously. Serious times would be his eventually, but they were not his lot just yet.

"It is not that I could not do the calculation. It is that I did not wish to do it," Graeme replied. "The other one," he whispered to Bea.

"Are you cheating?" Everett asked.

"I am merely attempting to assure myself of a better position from which to beat you."

Everett turned toward his brother, who was still leaning over Bea's shoulder, whispering in her ear. His brow furrowed as he took in the way the two were cozily positioned.

"Yes," he said slowly as if distracted, "but are you cheating?"

Graeme smiled at his brother's expression. It was good to see him finally taking notice of Bea, even if it was only because Graeme was nearly cheek to cheek with her.

"Mr. Clayton –"

"Graeme," Graeme hissed in Bea's ear.

"Mr. Clayton," she said firmly, "does not cheat. Cheating is for a much weaker sort of man, is it not, Mr. Clayton?"

Graeme nearly forgot himself and gave her cheek a brushing kiss when she turned her head, but he caught himself in time not to embarrass her. He could have withstood the teasing he would have received, but he would never do anything to harm Bea.

"Indeed, it is. I do not play games of shifting and shadows." At least not often. He straightened and smiled at Miss Love. That lady seemed the continually shadowy sort.

He had heard her name bandied around his club as coquettish and a likely candidate to be lead astray in some dark corner. In his opinion, she was not the sort of lady after whom a soon-to-be-parson should be chasing. No, Everett would do better with a lady of Bea's quality. He should probably take his brother aside and inform him of the things he knew about the lovely Miss Love, and perhaps he would — after their guests left.

For now, he would continue as he was, attempting, with little success, to get his brother to notice Bea while enjoying spending so much time at her side.

Chapter 4

BEA SIGHED AS SHE watched a drop of rain trail down the windowpane. Usually, she did not mind rainy days, for after her work was done, she would sneak up to the old schoolroom where she could paint, read, or simply sit at the window and watch the world get washed clean of the past and made ready for the new growth that would follow the rain. However, today, she would be expected to help entertain her cousins, and both Grace and Felicity had already grumbled several times about not being able to go on the picnic that had been planned.

The sky was growing darker, and the light for working on her stitching was fleeting, so Beatrice tucked the sash she wished to add to her yellow dress back into her workbasket. Michaelmas and its assembly were yet six weeks away. There was no need to strain her eyes to adorn her dress when there would be an ample amount of sunny days between now and then to complete the pattern she had begun.

"Oh, la," Grace said dolefully.

Bea closed her eyes and drew a calming breath in preparation for whatever complaint she was about to hear. Then, she fixed a smile on her face as she lifted her eyes from her workbasket to her cousin.

"I had such hopes of visiting the meadow." Grace rose and walked to the window where Bea sat. "Mr. Everett Clayton described it so well that I am certain I have never seen anything so lovely in all my life."

"We picnicked there the last time you were here." Bea kept her voice soft in an attempt to mollify some of Grace's disappointment and hopefully, prevent another declaration about how hideous it was that it was raining on a day when the delight of a picnic was anticipated.

"Oh, but I am certain it has changed so much in two years that I shall not recognize it. Things are that way, you know." Grace pulled her eyes away from the greyness of the day and turned them toward her cousin. "When you see them all the time, you forget how much they have changed and how delightful they can be." She sighed and sat down next to Bea. "I am certain I shall find it much altered."

Bea could not help smiling at the forlorn look on Grace's face and the wistful tone of her voice. She sounded very much like a young girl, and Bea found she could not fault

Grace for being unable to contain her disappointment as she should. Grace was, after all, merely seventeen, and not all ladies matured so quickly as Bea had, especially not ladies who still had both their mother and their father to dote on them.

"Beatrice likes to paint on rainy days," Mrs. Tierney offered.

Bea could tell by the tightness of her mother's expression that having young ladies around who were not averse to grumbling and complaining was beginning to wear on her. Neither Bea nor Max had ever been the sort of children to carry on about a disappointment for long.

"There are supplies in the schoolroom." Mrs. Tierney suggested, her smile softening as she looked at her daughter. "Although Beatrice has not had a lesson in almost two years, I cannot bring myself to redo the room just yet, and so it remains, waiting to be used on days like today."

Bea caught her frown before her mother could see it. Her father had insisted that the schoolroom be made up specifically for Bea, and she was loath to share it. It was her room, her bastion of solitude. However, she knew sharing her personal refuge would benefit not only her cousins but also her mother, and bringing pleasure to her mother was not something Bea would refuse to do. Therefore, with more excitement than she felt at the prospect, she agreed with her mother and insisted that her cousins join her in painting.

"Max will return soon," Mrs. Tierney added encouragingly. "I am certain he would be willing to sit for a silhouette or a portrait."

This brought a delighted squeal from Grace. "Felicity is the very best at taking likenesses. Mr. Bailey complimented her on her work all the time when she was at school and even used one of her pieces to demonstrate how a likeness should be done."

To Bea, it appeared that, according to Grace, Felicity was always the best at one thing or another. Felicity's samplers were the best and most elaborate. Felicity knew just the right ribbon to add to a hat to make it the envy of her friends. Felicity had the best taste in gowns and music. It was most frustrating! Bea sighed softly and directed her frustration to carefully organizing her work basket before tucking it away and leading her cousins to the schoolroom and seeing that they had everything they needed to be entertained.

Then, as Felicity and Grace chattered about some roses that were prized for their colour, Bea got out her landscape and set out her own painting supplies.

"Oh, those are lovely," Grace said, coming to look inside the wooden box of brushes that had been a gift from Lady Clayton to Bea on her last birthday. "These are nearly as nice as the ones Miss Abernathy has, Felicity." Grace turned to her sister. "Come, take a look. You will like them."

Felicity's left brow rose, and her lips pursed in an expression that declared she certainly could not be bothered to cross the room to look at a set of anything.

"A brush is a brush. It is not the tools that make the artist great but the technique the artist uses and the talent she possesses. I tell that to Amelia — Miss Abernathy —" she explained to Bea, "all the time. And truly, Grace, it is not as if Amelia can paint better because of her brushes. She possesses no talent. Her work is still dreadful. It is fortunate she is so skilled at playing the harp and dancing, or she would be in a sorry state. What man would wish to marry a lady with no accomplishments whatsoever?"

"One who wishes for her thirty thousand, I suppose," replied Grace, causing both herself and her sister to titter.

"Is Miss Abernathy someone from your school?" Bea asked in an attempt to participate in her cousins' conversation.

"Oh, she is my dearest friend," Felicity said. "We were in school together, and now we attend all the soirees together. We are nearly inseparable. In fact, I have missed her dreadfully these past weeks."

Bea tipped her head and studied her painting, deciding both where to put some flowers and how her cousin could speak as she was about Miss Amelia Abernathy and yet claim to be her particular friend. This was why it was challenging to participate in discussions with her cousins.

Their ways were so foreign to her. "When will you see her again?"

"Oh, in a fortnight. When we leave here, we are to travel to her father's home in Kent for a house party. It will be very exciting. We might even both find a husband while we are there," Felicity replied.

"If we both still require one," Grace whispered with a knowing smile.

Felicity's cheeks coloured as she glanced at Bea and then gave her sister a sharp look.

Bea picked up her brush and attempted to ignore the implication of Grace's words. Everett had been most attentive to Felicity for the past five days since their first introduction. He had walked with her, played cards with her, sang while she played the piano, and even taken Bea's book of verses to read to Felicity.

Bea made a show of concentrating on the flowers she was planting in the garden on her canvas, and said, "A house party will be exciting, I am sure."

"Oh, indeed!" Grace exclaimed before beginning a litany of things that she just knew would happen at this party. This, in turn, led into another recital of many of the interesting bits of gossip from the season. This meandering stream of stories, which were of great interest to the Misses Loves and of little interest to Beatrice, continued until there was a soft tapping at the door and in walked Max, followed closely by Everett and Graeme.

A story about an unfortunate gentleman who had been rejected twice by the same lady ended abruptly and was replaced with excited exclamations of greeting and cries of how dreadfully dull the day had been without the gentleman for company.

"Did you miss me?" Graeme asked Bea. He had wandered away from the shrill voices of the Misses Loves and had found his way to the corner where Bea was working.

"It is a fine representation," he said as he studied her painting. "You are becoming quite proficient in landscapes, which means you will soon have to move on to other things such as handsome neighbours whom you missed." And who had missed her.

As he settled himself against the wall just behind her and to her left, he had to admit how pleasant it was to be greeted by her smile. He had been restless all day, but here, he finally felt at ease.

Bea chuckled. "Did I miss you?"

"Oh, you did," Graeme replied with a smile. "I hear it was quite dull around here without me."

Beautiful blue eyes filled with amusement met his.

"Most dreadfully, but if you do not believe me, you may ask Grace."

How his brother could prefer anyone to Bea was baffling.

"There is no need for her to repeat it. I heard her quite well when we arrived," he replied with a laugh.

Max kissed his sister on the cheek in greeting. "I have put the thread you wanted into your workbasket, and this is the book you wished to borrow." He placed it on the table next to her. "Everett apologized for not returning it when he was finished reading it yesterday."

"I did not realize he needed to apologize to you," Bea said with a raised brow.

So, his brother's actions were beginning to vex the ever-patient Bea? Graeme turned his eyes toward his brother to watch him as he was still being regaled by the Miss Loves about something.

"He was not apologizing to me, ninny," Max said. "He was sending his apologies to you."

"He could not walk across the room and make them himself?" Graeme's voice was thick with contempt. "I shall speak to him," he promised.

His brother had been raised with better manners than he was currently demonstrating and the fact that it was Bea whom he was treating so poorly made it a far greater offense in Graeme's mind. Bea was not just some lady. Her care had been entrusted to their father.

"There is no need," Bea assured him. "I am certain Everett will remember to speak to me at some point."

Graeme nodded toward his brother, who was still engrossed in whatever it was that Felicity was showing him. Their heads were bent together over something. "Has he been like this the whole time I was gone?"

Graeme had left two days ago, to visit a good friend and help him with the purchase of a horse, and had only returned that morning.

"Like what?" Max asked. "Swooning at my cousin's feet?"

"Yes, that," Graeme replied, "and doing it to the exclusion of all else."

Max shrugged.

"Yes." Bea's answer was soft and worryingly resigned.

"We expect a happy announcement any day now," Max said with a laugh.

Graeme glanced at Bea, who was applying herself to her work with fierce determination. It was a sign that she was not at all happy. He had worried that leaving Stratsbury was a bad idea, but he had promised Shelton that he would accompany him to get that horse. Now, Graeme knew that he had been correct, and the person, whom he had hoped to help see happy, was far from it.

"It has not progressed to that in so short a time, has it?" he asked.

Bea lifted one shoulder and let it fall.

"Are you well?" Max asked, finally noticing his sister's distraught look.

Bea smiled brightly at her brother, but it was a forced brightness.

"I am well," she assured him. "Rainy days tend to make me quiet. You know this, and you must also remember that I have been listening to our cousins all day. My ears are weary."

It was more than weary ears. It appeared to Graeme that his dear friend had a weary heart as well. Had she truly given up all hope where Everett was concerned?

"Do you need a rest?" Max pressed. "Graeme, Everett, and I can entertain Felicity and Grace while you go lie down."

"I am well," Bea insisted. "Mama will call for tea now that you are home, and I shall stay behind to work up here. A few moments of silence and my spirits shall be restored."

Graeme doubted that last bit, and from the look on Max's face, her brother was not convinced either.

"If you are certain," Max agreed uneasily.

"I am."

"Very well. Then, I shall see if tea is being made ready and return. Shall I fetch you a cup?"

"That will not be necessary," said Graeme. "I will bring her one when I get mine." He tipped his head and raised a shoulder in a half-shrug in answer to Max's startled look. "I, too, find your cousins grating, and I might not be able to refrain from speaking harshly to my halfwit brother. Therefore, it might be best if I invade Bea's solitude."

While it was true that he had no desire to listen to the Miss Loves, he also did not wish to leave Bea. He needed to see her smile. He turned toward her and placed a hand on his heart. "I promise to invade your solitude quietly."

An actual smile, not a forced one, curled Bea's lips while delight shone in her eyes, and Graeme knew in that instant he would promise just about anything to see that expression always on her face. She was a dear friend, after all, and he always wished to see his friends happy. Therefore, it was only natural that he should feel so about Bea, or so he told himself in an attempt to reason away the startling thought.

"Are you certain you are not courting my sister?" Max asked with a grin. "I would not mind, you know."

Bea rolled her eyes and shook her head.

"I do not think she would have me," Graeme said with a smile on his lips and an odd ache in his chest.

"Well," Max said as he turned to leave, "if she ever changes her mind, you have my permission to court her, and I am confident I could persuade Mother that you are not a complete reprobate."

"Lying is not becoming," Graeme said to Max's back.

"You are not a reprobate," Bea said.

"I am not?" Graeme pulled a chair over near her and sat down. "It is very disappointing to hear I have not succeeded since I have tried so hard to be one."

"No gentleman with a heart so good and kind as yours could ever be termed a reprobate." Bea looked over at him and, seeing him sitting in a chair that was designed for someone much younger and shorter than he, giggled. He could not blame her. He was certain he did look ridiculous since his knees were nearly as high as his chest.

"There are other chairs," she suggested.

"Not over here," he answered. He was not leaving her side until he was required to gather their tea. "You think I am kind?"

"I do."

"I shall have to work on that," he muttered in a light-hearted tone.

"Please do not." Bea turned towards him for a moment. "I like that you are kind — and honest and occasionally polite." Mischief twinkled in her eyes.

He shrugged. "I will allow it to be so, but only if you promise not to tell anyone else. We rogues have an image to maintain."

"I promise to not say a word," Bea agreed with a laugh.

"Everett," Graeme called, "you should come see Bea's picture. It is nearly complete, and I think she has captured the meadow nearly to perfection."

He heard Bea's small, displeased gasp. She would likely be rather put out with him for drawing attention to her work and complimenting it. But her painting was good, and his brother had yet to even extend a polite greeting to her. And that last fact was one Graeme wished to see corrected immediately. He was not unaware of the hurt such neglect had caused Bea.

"You are painting the meadow?" Grace asked.

"I am."

"Has she truly captured it?" Grace turned to Everett.

"I said she did," Graeme muttered.

"A few more flowers, and it will be very like how I remember it," Everett said with a smile. "It is very good."

"Thank you," Bea murmured.

"She was also grateful to have her book returned." Graeme tapped the book that lay on the table and glared at his brother.

"Was that your book that Mr. Everett Clayton was reading to us?" Felicity asked.

"It is not mine, but it is one I had borrowed and had not finished reading," Bea explained.

"I am sorry I forgot to return it," Everett said with a sheepish grin.

"I am happy that you did not forget longer," Bea replied. "I am looking forward to finishing it."

An odd sense of pride swelled in Graeme's chest at her words, and he felt a desire to congratulate her for not just brushing the apology aside with an "It is of little significance." He knew, from the way her cheeks flushed, that replying as she had done was not easily accomplished.

"I thank you for being so understanding," Everett replied, shifting as if he were going to lean against the table and begin a conversation.

"Let me take your likeness," Felicity suggested, placing a hand on Everett's arm and drawing his attention away from Bea. "I am very good at it," she coaxed.

"Oh, she is," Grace assured and then, as they moved away, continued on with the same information she had shared with Mrs. Tierney about the instructor who used Felicity's work as an example to instruct others.

"He is an idiot," Graeme grumbled. "So easily led by a pair of fine eyes and ample —" Graeme coughed as he realized what he was going to say about Felicity's figure was perhaps not appropriate to be saying to Bea.

Bea smiled sadly. "I am beginning to agree."

It had indeed come to that. She was giving up on Everett.

"Ah, but they will be leaving in ... what? Surely, it is soon, is it not?"

As disappointed as he was with his brother, he could not help but push his frustration to the side and attempt to lift her spirits. He truly did not know what she saw in his brother. She deserved better. She deserved someone who would not ignore her or place her behind another.

"Ten days," Bea said with a sigh.

"And then, he will return to himself," Graeme said it hopefully, but he knew that ten days was a long period of time when desires were stirred, and hopes, such as Miss Love appeared to have for his brother, were ignited.

Bea nodded, though to Graeme it appeared she was only placating him to leave the subject of Everett behind, and continued mingling small white and yellow flowers with the blue ones that were already in the scene.

Chapter 5

FOR TWO DAYS, THE clouds prevailed in the sky, spitting out the occasional burst of rain — sometimes soft and gentle and other times as if someone in the heavens had kicked over a mop bucket. The greyness of the days and the dampness of the ground kept Bea and her cousins indoors.

For those same two days, Heathcote was blessed with the presence of the Clayton brothers. One came to sit for and fawn over Felicity, and the other, to watch and grumble.

So it was, on the day when the skies finally cleared, that the cloudless sky was greeted by Beatrice with some relief, for now, they could take their drawing and painting into the sunshine where Grace's exclamations of delight, over the drawing her sister was doing, could reverberate off of the trees and flowers, rather than the walls of the schoolroom, which had become to be a very constraining room with so many people of a talkative variety to fill it.

Then came the joyful day two days later when the ground was declared to have sufficiently dried out, and it was decided they would pack up their art supplies, along with a picnic lunch, and finally seek out the meadow Grace so desired to see.

On this morning, as her cousins eagerly awaited the arrival of the Claytons, Bea handed her bag of drawing supplies to her brother, who stored them in the carriage next to the picnic basket.

"Are you not bringing your paints?" he asked.

Bea shook her head. "I prefer to draw when in the meadow and paint when in the house." She drew in a deep breath and released it with satisfaction. "It is a beautiful day, is it not?"

"I will not argue that," Max replied. "I am pleased to see you looking so happy. I dare say you were beginning to look a bit wane by last evening."

Bea wrapped her arm around his and walked with him back toward the house.

"Today, I shall be able to find a quiet spot," she said, laying her head against his shoulder for a moment.

She loved moments of solitude. They refreshed her as nothing else could. Usually, she would find a few moments each day to steal away to the schoolroom, her bedroom, or some corner in the garden, but since her cousins had arrived, finding both those moments and any place that was not invaded either by person or voice had been nearly impossible. There had been a few times of refreshment during their visits to Stratsbury when she was left to herself in the garden or in the library. However, they had not ventured from Heathcote in four days, and Bea's equanimity was wearing thin.

"Whatever the reason, I am glad to see your improvement. Perhaps we will be able to arrange the drives so that you can even enjoy a bit of quiet while travelling. You look tired."

Bea sighed. "I am. I must admit I have not slept well, but I suspect today will help with that as well."

Lying upon her bed at night had been the only place where she had been able to contemplate the events of the day, which was as necessary for Bea as eating or getting fresh air. However, her ruminations had not all been of the particularly pleasant sort. There was no denying in her mind that things were progressing between Felicity and Everett to a point from which there was no turning aside of affections. And so, she had begun to prepare herself for the inevitable disappointment.

She tugged gently on her brother's arm, causing him to stop. They were nearing the house, and she needed to speak to him where her cousins could not hear. Her heart seemed to leap into her throat, but there was something she needed to ask him — no matter how distressing his answer might be.

"I have listened to our cousins speak endlessly of their desires to marry." Her cheeks grew rosy. It felt wrong to be asking what she was, but she reminded herself that it was only information for her own sake and not gossip that she sought.

Max tipped his head. His brow furrowed in question. "I do not plan to ask either of our cousins to marry me if that is what is worrying you. I know Grace has batted her lashes at me and all that, but I have not developed a fondness for her."

Bea smiled. She had been wondering about that, almost as much as she had been wondering about Everett's intentions. "They have spoken most frequently about Felicity's hopes." The fingers of her free hand ran back and forth along the seam of her gown nervously. "Does she hope in vain?"

Her brother's cheeks puffed out for a moment before he blew out a breath. "Everett has not mentioned his intentions, but he seems smitten."

She swallowed the disappointment that rose at such a statement. After all, she had known that it was not just a trick of her mind making her see how enamoured Everett was with Felicity. "Do you expect him to offer for her?"

Max shrugged. "I am not certain, but I would not be surprised should it happen." His eyes narrowed as he studied her face. "You do not still like him, do you?"

Max had found Bea's diary about four years ago and had read her confessions of love for Everett Clayton.

She had been embarrassed then to have him know about her infatuation, and, to be honest, she still was. She was not entirely sure how she felt about Everett at the moment. Did she like him? Yes. Did she want to admit it aloud? No. So instead, she lifted and lowered one shoulder in a half-shrug and allowed that to be her reply.

Max sighed and pulled her into his embrace. "Do you wish for me to speak to him?"

"No," Bea said with some force. "He must not know."

Max released her and, placing her hand in the crook of his arm again, began a short circuit of the drive rather than returning directly to the house. "I could –"

"No," Bea interrupted. "I only wished to know so I can prepare myself."

Max stopped and stood for a moment, silently shaking his head. "If I had known you still harboured feelings for him, I could have arranged things, made comments, promoted you." His eyes shimmered when he turned to her. "You know I would do anything to see you happy and protect you from harm."

She nodded. Her lip trembled at seeing such emotion on her brother's face. "That is why I could not tell you," she whispered. "I am not the sort of lady who schemes and steals her way into a gentleman's affections."

"Ah, Bea." He wrapped an arm around her shoulder, and they continued walking. "Perhaps he is merely infatuated and having a bit of a flirt. It is a rather pleasant thing to be the object of a lady's attention."

"Perhaps he is," Bea agreed. "But I fear that even if it is just a passing fancy for him, Felicity seems determined to ensnare him."

Her brother blew out a breath. "I shall warn him if I can."

"Thank you," Bea wrapped her arm around his middle and squeezed him tightly. "Even if he is never to love me, I would hate to see him taken in." She sighed. "However, there is the possibility that Felicity might actually love him in earnest. Perhaps you should not say anything."

"I will only plant a seed of caution. I shall not accuse our cousin of anything heinous."

Bea squeezed him again. She was fortunate to have such a brother to whom she could speak so openly and who cared so well for her. Not everyone was so blessed.

"Here comes Clayton now," said her brother, nodding toward the road.

"Two carriages?" Bea asked in surprise. "Could they have not ridden together? And when did they get a curricle?"

Max waved vigorously at the approaching vehicles. "That is Shelton's curricle."

"Who is Mr. Shelton?" Bea asked a bit breathlessly. It seemed Max had forgotten she was still holding his arm, for his strides had lengthened, and she had to scamper to keep up.

"He is a friend of Graeme's — the fellow he went to visit about a horse. You remember that, do you not?"

"Max, please. Could we not assume a more sedate pace?" She pulled on his arm.

"My apologies," he muttered as he slowed.

Thankfully, they reached the steps before either vehicle did, and Bea was given a moment to bring her breathing back under control before having to make any greetings.

"She's quite the beauty, is she not?" Roger Shelton eased himself down next to Graeme, who was seated a short distance away from Bea.

Graeme had wanted to sit with Bea as she drew, but since that would likely mean Shelton would follow suit, he did not. He knew how Bea enjoyed drawing in quietness, and Shelton was not the quietest of gentlemen.

"Which one?" Graeme asked, sparing only a glance at his friend before returning his eyes to his book, which was propped in such a way that he could appear to be reading and yet steal glances at Bea.

She had looked well earlier, but yesterday, her features had been drawn and tired, causing him to worry that she was becoming unwell. Bea would never admit such a thing until it was beyond what was acceptable and the apothecary would have to be called. As odd as it was to imagine, he wished that she was the sort of lady who complained, but she was not.

"The one on your brother's arm."

"Ah, That is Miss Love. Did you not meet her in town at the Abernathy's soiree?"

Shelton snapped his fingers. "That's it! I have been attempting to place her all day. She is Amelia Abernathy's friend." He tipped his head. "I am surprised that she did not latch on to you instead of your brother. I heard she was looking for money."

Graeme shrugged. "I heard the same, but I was not here when she arrived." He shifted and closed his book. "She had my brother well enchanted before I appeared. Not that I would have allowed her sort to cling to me anyway."

"Her sort?' Shelton asked with a laugh. "When did you become so discriminating in your tastes? There was a time when a pretty face and a pleasing figure was all that was needed to catch your interest."

Graeme huffed and shook his head. "Not if they were the sort to cry compromise, which she is. Besides, I do not like her — not even well enough for a dalliance."

Shelton's brows rose in surprise. "Your brother seems to like her quite well."

"I also do not like that," Graeme replied firmly. "I have warned him, but you know Everett."

Shelton nodded. "He tends to think he is always right."

"Precisely so."

"Do you think he genuinely likes her?"

Graeme sighed. "Yes. I have considered the possibility." As much as he wished with all his heart that Everett was merely being duped, he could not deny that his brother seemed truly besotted and not just a complete fool. He stole a look at Bea. He had still not reasoned out how his brother could prefer Miss Love over Bea.

"She is a pretty thing as well," Shelton whispered as he indicated Bea with a nod of his head.

"Why are you whispering?" Graeme demanded as a quiver of irritation at the comment settled in his gut.

"I do not want her brother to hear me say such a thing. He seemed rather protective of her when I was introduced."

Graeme chuckled. "Your reputation precedes you, my friend. Any brother with half an ounce of sense would be protective of a pretty sister around you. I swear you reek of charm and seduction."

Shelton shrugged and looked quite pleased with himself. "I do, do I not? But then, so do you — or at least you used to. However, there is something different about you today. You are shunning pretty girls and keeping watch over her." Again, he indicated Bea with a nod of his head. "Is she special?"

Graeme smiled and nodded. "She's Bea."

"I am afraid I do not follow."

"Her father and mine were good friends since childhood, and to make a long and tediously boring tale short, ten years ago, when Bea was nine and Max was sixteen, their father, Captain Tierney, moved them to Heathcote. He left shortly after they were settled and never returned — killed by the Spanish or the French, I do not know which one, since it is hard to tell the nationality of a bullet. My father had promised that if such a thing were to happen, he would see to the care of the captain's family."

"So, she is like a sister then?"

Graeme shook his head. "No, not a sister. A friend." A very dear friend, he added to himself. "She likes my brother," Graeme blurted. "She has for some time." He huffed. It was a sound of exasperation. "I have attempted to draw his attention away from Miss Love to Bea, but he is too besotted." He shook his head. "He is going to break Bea's heart, and I could throttle him for it."

Shelton's eyes were wide, and his eyebrows raised in surprise.

"Bea is quiet and all that is good. She is kind and helpful. She never wishes for praise but always wishes to please. She would make a perfect parson's wife, but my brother is too stupid to recognize her worth."

"Are you certain you do not think of her as a sister? For you speak like a brother or –" Shelton tilted his head and studied his friend. "You love her."

Graeme's brow furrowed, and he shook his head in disbelief. "Of course, I love her. She's Bea." He moved to rise, but Shelton's hand on his arm stopped him.

"No, not as a friend. She's the one you spoke about when you visited, is she not?"

Graeme blew out a breath and turned to face his friend. "Bea loves my brother, and I only wish to see her happy." No matter how the idea of his brother marrying Bea irritated him! She deserved better than a dolt who had to be convinced of her worth rather than recognizing it of his own volition.

Shelton nodded his head slowly as if he were considering what Graeme was saying, but Graeme knew better. Shelton was reasoning things out, piecing things together, and drawing conclusions. A gentleman did not survive as somewhat of a rake and be generally well-liked, as Shelton had, without a keen mind.

"She loves my brother," Graeme repeated.

It had been foolish of him to speak to Shelton about a lady whom he found enchanting but who was unavailable.

However, his tongue had been loosened by alcohol that night after they had ridden out to purchase Shelton's new hunter, and the things that Graeme had been pondering since the evening he had nearly kissed Bea during that blasted card game had come spilling out. He had been wise enough to leave out names, but still, he knew Shelton was no fool.

"Do you truly wish to see her happy?"

Graeme looked at Shelton warily. "Yes."

Shelton smiled. "Then, capture her heart before your brother can break it."

The hairs on the back of Graeme's neck bristled. The smile Shelton was wearing was calculating. He had seen it before — often right before some poor chap was about to be fleeced or lose his lady.

"I consider myself the charitable sort," Shelton continued, "and I am approaching that age where a wife will be expected. I could save her heart from harm."

Graeme's eyes narrowed. "You will stay away from her," he growled.

Shelton chuckled, clearly enjoying taunting his friend. "Will you call me out if I do not?"

Graeme folded his arms and smirked in return. Shelton knew that Graeme would never call anyone out because, for one thing, it was illegal, and for another, Graeme was not the best shot nor all that adept with a sword. So, to use a duel as a threat would be of no effect. However, there was a threat that Graeme knew would shake Shelton. "No, I will shoot your horse."

Shelton chuckled again. "Very well, I will not risk my horse unless I see it is necessary to do so." He rose. "However, I think I shall see what Miss Tierney has been drawing — just in the way of being friendly and all. Would you care to join me?"

"Did you say you were returning home tonight?" Graeme asked hopefully as he scrambled to his feet.

Shelton shook his head. "No, your mother said that I may stay the week. She is a dear, is she not?"

"I promise you that I will shoot your horse," Graeme grumbled as he followed Shelton over to where Bea was sitting.

Chapter 6

"HAVE A GO, MISS Tierney." Mr. Shelton held out his racket to Bea. "Miss Grace has already outdone me three times. I am rather fatigued." He smiled and wiggled the racket in invitation. "Your brother says you are quite good at this game."

"Go on, Bea," Max encouraged, as he dropped onto the bench next to his sister. "Neither Shelton nor I have been able to beat her. You are our only hope to dethrone Grace as queen of the shuttlecock."

"Can Grace and Felicity not play each other?" Bea asked. She had been riding earlier that day, and, with the weather being so warm, she was feeling the first pangs of a headache. A rest would likely drive those pains away while a vigorous game would not.

"Felicity will not play anyone who does not bear the last name Clayton," Mr. Shelton grumbled.

"No matter how loudly anyone bearing that name protests," Max added.

Bea had heard Graeme's grousing. "It does appear that Mr. Clayton is in a rather foul mood."

Max chuckled. "I am impressed that he has not yet stomped off in a huff."

Mr. Shelton eased down onto the bench beside Max. "He'll endure for as long as he feels there might be a hope of victory. Loss never sits well with him — a loss to a lady sits even less well."

Though Max had informed Bea about Mr. Shelton's reputation for charming ladies, he seemed to her to be a gentleman of worth, for he had treated her very respectfully and he showed such fondness for his friend. Anyone who was a particular friend of Graeme's could not be a complete ne'er-do-well, for Graeme did not abide fools and charlatans.

Max took the racquet Shelton still held and passed it to Bea. "One game," he begged. "Losing to a female does not sit well with any gentleman, and begging his sister to take up his defense is not easily done. Please, take pity on us and defend our honour." He clasped his hands in front of him and turned doleful eyes to her.

"You are pitiful." Bea laughed as she rose. "I shall do my best to restore your honour." She curtseyed deeply to the gentlemen on the bench. "I do hope there is a reward for such valiant behaviour."

The shuttlecock bounced off the lawn. Everett had missed hitting it, and once again, Felicity had won a point.

Since the method of play, as set forth by the Miss Loves, required whoever had dropped the shuttlecock to bow out of the game and be replaced by the third person standing at the side, Graeme took the racquet his brother handed him and, with a sigh, prepared to enter the game.

The same process had been followed in the second group, which had been made up of Shelton, Max, and Grace until Shelton and Max had deserted him. He would have gladly joined them in departing if he could have done so without admitting utter defeat at the hand of a lady like Felicity Love. Had he been playing against Miss Grace, he could have born the defeat, but there was something about Miss Love that provoked him to the point of caring that she would be named the ultimate victor.

"Beatrice," Grace cried warmly.

Graeme looked in the direction Miss Grace was. There was Bea with a racquet in her hand. This game just might become fun if Bea was playing.

"Have you seen how many times Felicity has retained her racquet?" Grace asked.

"I have, and my brother and Mr. Shelton have begged me to play in their stead. I understand they have been unsuccessful in causing you to surrender your racquet and hoped I might do better."

Graeme guffawed. "Do not tell me that Shelton and Max wish for you to defend their honour?"

"Men are such delicate creatures." She wore a teasing smile. "Their spirits are so easily crushed, and their moods so easily fouled –" one eyebrow arched "– that one must do all one can to protect them."

"We are not delicate creatures," Graeme protested. His mood was foul, he would not deny that, but he was not a delicate creature. He had not quit the game. "Do you hear her, Everett? Bea is condemning all men just because Shelton and Max are not up to the challenge of winning. Shocking, is it not?"

Bea's cheeks turned rosy at his teasing, but she did not shy away or attempt to turn the conversation. She was in the game to win.

Everett chuckled. "No, it is not so very shocking, considering it is Bea."

"Whatever do you mean?" Bea asked with feigned innocence.

"You may be quiet and bookish, but you are also devilishly determined once you have set your mind to a task. She is a fearsome opponent, Miss Grace," Everett warned.

How could his brother know such things about Bea and not love her for it?

"Bea?" Grace's eyes were wide. "I cannot imagine her being anything but sweet and obliging."

"Oh, she is that," Everett assured. "Bea is one of the sweetest and most obliging ladies you will ever meet unless she has a mallet or a racquet in her hand."

"Or a set of cards," Graeme added. Bea's eyes lowered as they often did when people talked about her in any flattering fashion. It, much like the teasing smile she had turned on him just moments ago, was one of the many expressions that he found particularly charming about Bea. "And it was Bea who rounded the tree first this morning on our ride," he added.

"She beat Shelton?" Everett asked in surprise. He had not gone riding with his brother, Shelton, and Max, because Felicity was fearful of horses. Instead, he and she had remained behind at Stratsbury with Grace, who was to act as a chaperone for their walk through the gardens and down the lane.

"Just, but beat him she did."

"He was being gentlemanly," Bea argued. "I am certain he could have won if he was only riding against other gentlemen."

Graeme and Everett both laughed at that.

"Shelton is rarely a gentleman," Graeme said.

"I cannot believe that. He has been all that is proper whenever we are together."

A disturbing thought crossed Graeme's mind. There was only one time when Shelton would play the gentleman and allow a lady to win at anything.

"I assure you that it is true. He dislikes losing just as much as you do."

He glanced over to where Shelton was conversing with Max. Shelton had best not be attempting to win Bea's affections.

"We have just met. He was likely trying to make a good first impression. The next ride might be different."

"The next ride?" Graeme's head snapped back around to the group gathered around him.

"Yes, on the day after tomorrow, if the weather holds, we are to meet for a ride. Max thought two days of riding in a row might be too much for me." Bea added the last part quietly.

Graeme scowled. Shelton had not mentioned such an arrangement to him. He would make certain he was also part of that ride. Shelton was not going to woo Bea without some interference.

"Must we discuss riding any longer?" Felicity asked. "Can we not play?"

"We have no one to take the place of whoever drops the shuttlecock," said Grace.

"Oh, I had only planned on playing one game," Bea explained. "The weather is warm, and my head is a trifle sore."

Graeme eyed her carefully, looking for any signs that she was unwell. The fact that Bea had mentioned any matter, whether trifling or not, was, in his opinion, a reason to worry. She looked well enough.

"The winner of your game could play the winner of ours," he offered. "That is if Bea thinks she can tolerate two games."

Grace gasped indignantly. "She has not won yet."

"Oh, but she will," Graeme muttered. Then, he turned to Felicity. "What say you, Miss Love? If you win this match, which I am not saying you will, are you agreeable to playing Bea," he smiled and, after a short pause, added, "or your sister."

"And the winner of that game could play me," Everett added.

"I will gladly play you," Graeme said to Everett.

"You?" Felicity tittered. "You have not done very well at beating me yet today, and to play your brother, you shall not only have to beat me but also either Beatrice or Grace."

"Ah, but, to this point, the prize was not to play Bea," he replied.

Bea rolled her eyes. "I am beginning to regret agreeing to play for Mr. Shelton and Max."

"But you have agreed," said Everett. "The winner of your match will play the winner of this match, and then that person shall play me."

"And then we shall have tea and lounge about until it is time for dinner," Graeme added.

"Very well," Bea said, turning to Grace. "You may hit first."

They took their places, but instead of both teams playing at the same time as they had before, Graeme insisted that he and the others watch Grace and Bea play before playing their own match. Felicity only grumbled slightly before allowing that Everett was likely correct in agreeing with his brother. Graeme was just thankful that he could arrange a short rest period for Bea between games, and he was pleased to be able to watch her play, for her naturally retiring nature was replaced by determination once she entered the game.

The shuttlecock flew back and forth. Both ladies ran this way and that to hit it back to their opponent. However, after several minutes, the shuttlecock hit the ground and the round was over.

"Did I not say she would win?" Graeme could not help how the pride he felt at Bea's accomplishment coloured his tone.

Her flushed cheeks deepened in colour, and she dipped a curtsey in acceptance of his praise before taking her seat on the lawn next to Grace and Everett.

"Wish me well," Graeme said to her as he rose.

"May the best player win," she replied.

He could tell by her expression that she expected him to be annoyed that she had not sent him off to be victorious. But instead of kissing her lips, which were puckered to hold back her smile, as he surprisingly felt compelled to do, he merely bowed to her with a flourish and said, "Indeed, he shall."

Much to his delight, her smile spread across her face at his actions, and he entered this match against Felicity with more interest than he had for any game he had played yet today.

When play began, Grace and Everett cheered for Felicity to win, as Graeme expected. Bea, on the other hand, held her peace until he narrowly escaped missing a volley. Then, she clapped her hands and shouted a well done.

Delight buoyed his spirits, and he gave the shuttlecock a resounding thwack, sending it flying out of Felicity's reach. He turned and bowed to his audience of three.

"Miss Tierney," he said, extending his hand, "I believe this game is ours."

"So, it is," Bea said as she allowed him to help her to her feet. Then, she took her place and play began. It was not a short game. For though Graeme was finding it challenging to keep his eyes where they should be, since Bea was far more delightful to look at than some feathered object, he managed to school himself well enough to send many returning volleys.

"Oooh," Bea cried and went sprawling on the grass with the shuttlecock lying just in front of her racquet.

Graeme's breath left him in a whoosh. Dropping his racquet, he hurried to her side.

"Blast," she muttered as she pulled herself up to a sitting position.

"Careful! Do not rush in rising." He knelt next to her.

She huffed. "I am well. I am not happy, but I am well." She brushed at a few bits of grass that clung to her.

She was not well. If he had to guess how she was feeling, he would say she was put out that she had lost and likely embarrassed. Added to that, landing on the ground as she had surely hurt and... "Your arm is bleeding." Graeme pressed his handkerchief to the scrape just below her elbow on her right arm. "You should have let that one pass," he chided softly.

"And let you win?" She brushed at a tear that had escaped the blinking confines of her eyes.

"I won anyway," he said softly. He was rewarded with the small smile he sought.

"Is she injured?" Max appeared at Graeme's shoulder. "It was a spectacular move," he added as he crouched down next to his sister.

Graeme chuckled. "It was a very graceful leap." He lifted his handkerchief to examine her scrape. "We should see that this gets cleaned and dressed. Hold this." He once again pressed the cloth firmly against her still bleeding arm until her hand came to cover his. Then, he slipped his hand out from beneath hers and grabbed her right arm above her elbow as Max took her left arm, and together they helped her rise.

Bea grimaced as she rose, and she favoured one foot. She had hurt herself more than she was willing to admit. Why could she not complain just a bit?

"Did you turn your ankle?" Graeme swept her into his arms without waiting for her reply. He was not about to allow her to attempt walking and injure herself further.

"Yes," Bea admitted, "but I am certain that I can walk."

"You should not walk on it," Graeme replied.

"And that means that you must carry her?" Max asked. His eyes registered his shock at Graeme's holding his sister.

It had only seemed natural for Graeme to gather her into his arms when he saw her lips clench and her brow furrow as she tried to stand. Now, however, he supposed it did look odd that he should be assisting Bea, instead of allowing her brother to perform the duty.

"It is my doing," he explained. "I shall see her to the house as penance."

He waited, not breathing for a moment, until Max gave his approval. Graeme would have allowed Max to carry Bea if Max had insisted, of course, but he would not have been happy about relinquishing her. It felt good to have her here in his arms — exceptionally good — and, if he was to be honest with himself, it felt as if this was the place where she belonged.

Perhaps Shelton was correct. Perhaps he did need to win Bea's heart — not to protect it from being broken, but to protect his own heart from such a fate. Indeed, he could not imagine allowing another man — not his brother or even hers — rendering the service he was currently providing, for he could not countenance the idea of her in the arms of another — not now, not ever.

"I can walk," Bea protested. "My ankle is only a little sore. If you allowed me to lean on your arm, I am certain I could make it to the house without a problem."

"And how are you going to lean on my arm when your hand is required to press a cloth to your wound?" he asked as he began toward the house.

"I could tie the cloth around my arm."

He shook his head. "No, you must allow me to be the gallant knight."

She sighed. "I feel foolish."

"You should not," he answered, tightening his hold on her and pressing her closer to him. "You have saved me from playing another game."

She leaned her head against his shoulder. "You could have allowed me to win. Then you would not have had to play another game."

He chuckled. "I rarely allow anyone to win."

She laughed at the truth of his words. Anyone who knew him, knew that Graeme played to win — nearly always. There had only been a few times when he had willingly lost to his mother when playing cards.

"And you see where that gets you," she said. "Either playing more of a game which bores you or carrying foolish females around the garden."

"First," he replied, "I do not find the game as dull as the company I was forced to keep while playing, yourself excluded, of course. And second, I do not carry foolish females — ever. Had a foolish female fallen, I would have very ungallantly begged someone else to carry her or sent for a footman."

"Thank you. You always know what to say to make me feel better." She smiled up at him from where she rested against his shoulder. "You should know that the only other people who can do that are Max and my father."

He bowed his head in acceptance of her words. "I am honoured to be in such company." He gave her a squeeze. "And just like them, I would do anything to protect you."

Her head rubbed against his shoulder as she nodded. "I know," she whispered, and then silence fell comfortably around them as the truth of Graeme's statement settled into his heart and, he hoped, into hers as well.

Chapter 7

TWO DAYS LATER, GRAEME scanned the garden at Heathcote for Bea as he rode alongside Max and just behind Shelton. Today, Bea's mother had said she would be able to do more than sit on a sofa in the sitting room or a bench in the garden, and he knew she would take advantage of the freedom. She was not one who liked to be confined, but she also was not a disobedient daughter.

Her mother was not known to coddle her children, but she was also not the sort who foolishly flouted precautions, especially when it came to Beatrice. Having nearly lost her daughter to a fever when Bea was just eleven, Mrs. Tierney stuck firmly to all prescribed restrictions, and a turned ankle that showed signs of bruising required, according to Bea's mother, a full two days of rest with little walking. Mrs. Tierney would not confine Bea to her bed, but she would not have her hobbling about — not even with a cane. Bea was to rest with her foot on a pillow.

Ah! There she was, near the hedge, walking slowly and with a noticeable limp.

Shelton looked over his shoulder and smiled at Graeme before doffing his hat and greeting Bea. "Miss Tierney! I missed our rematch. I am confident I could have been victorious today."

The man was incorrigible! He had taunted Graeme about his carrying Bea to the house the day of the shuttlecock tournament and had not stopped being an annoyance ever since.

Bea hobbled over to the hedge which bordered the side of the garden and faced the path to the stables just as a groom came trotting up with a second at his heels.

"My mother was insistent that I should not ride, or I would have accompanied Max."

Shelton swung down from his horse. "I am certain it was a wise decision on her part, but yours was an absence which was felt most profoundly. May I join you for a walk around the garden?"

"I am only allowed one more circuit before I must sit and rest my foot."

"Then one escorted turn around the garden it will be." Shelton handed the reins of his horse to the groom and headed to the small opening in the hedge just a few feet away. "Do not move. Stay just where you are," he called as he went. "I shall be there directly."

Graeme's eyes narrowed as he watched Bea smile and welcome his friend.

"You look out of sorts," Max said as he dismounted.

"Do you not worry about how charming Shelton is being with your sister?" Graeme gave his horse's neck a pat before allowing a groom to lead him away.

"I see no harm in it. He will be gone in a few days, and I doubt he can do much damage in so little time." He smirked at Graeme. "Are you jealous?"

"No, I am not jealous. I am just well acquainted with my friend and his ways." It was not a complete lie. He was well acquainted with how Shelton conducted himself with females. It was, however, a complete and utter untruth that he was not jealous. He did not like the way Shelton was smiling at Bea or causing her to giggle. That was Graeme's job. He was the one who was supposed to tease her into a smile and shock her into laughter.

"He is flirting with Bea. Not some more easily duped young lady," Max replied.

His flirting with Bea was the point! It did not matter that Bea was more sensible than most ladies. Shelton knew that Graeme cared for her, and yet, the infuriating chap flirted despite that fact. Not that he was about to share any of those details with Max. Therefore, he clamped his teeth together and attempted to glare a hole through his friend as he followed Max through the hedge.

Thankfully, Shelton and Bea would not be allowed to walk so companionably for long, and he would not be the one to have to rouse suspicions further by being the interference. It was likely the first time since meeting them that Graeme was happy to see the Love sisters approaching from the house.

Everett was, of course, at Felicity's side. He had once again cried off riding to spend the morning with the ladies. For once, Graeme did not censure him for doing so, since he, himself, had wished to do the same thing.

"Mother said she would have breakfast set out on the terrace," Bea said as Max greeted her with a kiss on her cheek.

"Have you eaten?" He fell into step next to his sister.

"No, I was waiting for you, and you know I like to have some sort of exercise before breaking my fast. Even if that exercise is a very short and slow hobble around the garden."

"How is your ankle today?" Graeme flanked Shelton since both places next to Bea were already taken. "Is it enjoying the exercise as much as you are?"

Bea grimaced. "It is protesting loudly, but you must not tell my mother. I cannot bear another day of sitting."

"Bea may prefer to sit and read," Max said, "but she does not like to be required to sit and read."

That was excessively true. Bea was often in the company of a book. However, he had heard her grumbles over the years about the books her mother had prescribed as ones all young ladies should read. She had read them, but she had not enjoyed doing so.

"Who won the race today?" Felicity asked.

"I did," said Shelton, lifting his chin, puffing out his chest, and looking for all the world like the most pompous of gents.

The pose, however, was affected with a whimsical smile and air, for though Shelton was confident in his own abilities and person to the point of being obnoxious, he possessed not an arrogant bone in his body. It was this brashness, mixed with his natural charm, that made him popular with so many females.

Graeme's scowl deepened. It was a further reason that Bea should not be leaning on Shelton's arm.

"These gents were miles behind me," Shelton continued, looking at Graeme and raising a taunting brow while a smirk played at his lips. "I had half expected to be done with my breakfast before either of them rounded the tree and turned back to Heathcote."

"I should think not!" Max argued. "Graeme nearly overtook you at one point, and I was not so very far behind him."

"How exciting!" Grace chirped. "To the victor must go the spoils; therefore, Mr. Shelton shall have the first muffin!" She hurried over to the table that had been set out and lifted the cloth from the bowl of muffins, keeping the bowl in her possession until Shelton had seen Bea seated and taken his own seat. Only then did Grace hold out the muffins to him with a bit of a flourish, and after he had selected a nice plump cake from the top of the pile, she replaced the cloth and seated herself next to him.

Bea's lips twitched, and she shot a knowing glance toward Graeme. Grace had been arranging things so that she could be seated near Shelton ever since the day after their picnic — the day when she had played shuttlecock with him. It was obvious to anyone who was paying the smallest amount of attention that Grace was interested in capturing the gentleman's notice.

"Mr. Everett Clayton has been invited to the Abernathy's house party. Is that not the best news?" Grace said as she carefully sipped tea from her cup.

A breeze tugged at the cloths covering the food on the table as if it wished to make a plate of breakfast for itself. Bea's eyes turned toward Everett, whose cheeks had grown the faintest bit rosy.

"Is this good news?" Graeme asked his brother pointedly, not caring that it flustered him.

His heart did not know whether to rejoice at the news or be saddened. If his brother were gone, Graeme could have Bea all to himself and perhaps, convince her of his worth. However, he also knew that if Everett were delighted to attend a house party, he was very likely fully lost to Felicity. Such news would make Bea unhappy, and Graeme could not bear the thought of her being unhappy even if it would lead to his own happiness.

"It is not bad news. A house party is always a good time," Everett replied.

Graeme glanced at Bea and was relieved to see that she did not appear to be distressed by his brother's reply.

"Yes," Shelton agreed with a sly smile, "house parties can be a grand time as long as you avoid the true purpose of them."

Grace blinked. "Whatever do you mean?"

"He means he enjoys flirting but not enough to be leg-shackled," Graeme supplied.

Bea hid her smile behind her cup. It was good to see that he had shocked her into amusement.

"You do not wish to marry?" Grace asked, as if such an idea was the most ridiculous one in all the world.

"Grace," Felicity chided softly, though her eyes, unlike her tone, appeared eager to hear Shelton's answer to Grace's question.

"It is not that I do not wish to marry. It is just that I do not wish to marry at this particular time," Shelton said, as he picked a morsel of cake off his plate and popped it into his mouth. "There is plenty of time for marriage when I am older."

A bird song rang out from a branch of the tree overhead.

Shelton looked up. "Even the creatures agree, you see," he added with a smile.

Graeme settled back to watch the interaction between Shelton and Miss Grace. However, the reply to Shelton's comments did not come from the expected source.

"Do you fear it? Or is it just the giving up of freedom, which keeps you from marrying?" Bea's hand flew to her mouth. "Forgive me. That was most improper."

Graeme saw her cheeks redden. "Thinking aloud?" he asked. It was an unusual thing for Bea to speak without thought, and he could imagine how mortified she must be. He also wondered just how interested she was in his friend's marital state.

She nodded.

"So, Shelton, what is it?" Graeme asked. "Fear or freedom?"

"You do not need to answer." Bea shot Graeme a look of displeasure.

Graeme shrugged. "I am curious to hear his answer," he said with a smile. Perhaps if he could be more improper than she, it would lessen her mortification. However, from the look on her face, he was not certain that it was a good plan.

"I have no qualms about answering as long as every other person at the table answers as well," Shelton said. He held Graeme's gaze as if in challenge before he looked at each other person gathered at the table. Having received assurances of participation from Max, Everett, and the Miss Loves, he turned to Bea. "And you, Miss Tierney? Will you answer?"

"I will start if you wish."

He waved his right hand in such a fashion as to encourage her to continue.

"I am kept from the marital state by the lack of an offer," she said with a smile.

"Do you have a beau, who should be making this offer?" Shelton inquired.

Bea shook her head. "No, sadly, I do not."

"But you are not opposed to the idea of a beau or marriage, then?"

"No, Mr. Shelton, I am not. However, I do not wish for just any gentleman as a beau or husband. The gentleman, who wishes to marry me, must be of a good moral character and be someone whom I could love and respect and who would return those same feelings to me."

Shelton's eyes slid to Graeme and then returned to Bea. "That is very wisely said, Miss Tierney. I, too, would wish for love and respect in marriage."

"Yes, but that is not what keeps you from it, is it?" Graeme prodded. He did not like the way his friend was smiling at Bea nor the way Bea's eyes had dropped to her plate.

"No, it is not," Shelton replied, while shooing a fly away from his cup of tea before taking a sip. "I believe the question was if it was fear or freedom that kept me from marrying." He turned to Bea. "Would either of those keep you from marriage if there were a gentleman wishing to make an offer?"

"You are not offering, are you?' Max said with a grin.

"No, no, no. I am not ready to marry anyone even if she is as lovely as your sister or cousins. I was merely posing a question of interest." His eyes slid from Max's face to Graeme's. "For curiosity's sake." He smiled at Bea. "I have not offended you, have I?"

She shook her head. "No, I am not offended, nor am I so entrenched in my freedom, such that it is for a lady under the authority of her mother and brother, to refuse an offer if extended by a gentleman of good moral fiber, who would show me both love and respect." She gave Shelton a pointed look, and Graeme smiled at her temerity.

"Yes, yes, that is true, a young lady's freedom is not the same as that of a gentleman," Shelton acknowledged before Bea continued her answer.

"I do not fear marriage to such a man."

"Well said, Miss Tierney. Now, I shall answer." He took a sip of his tea and then drew a breath. Apparently, he was going to answer honestly. A flippant response would have slipped from Shelton much more easily.

Graeme looked from Shelton to Bea. Shelton was not the sort to be anything but open with those whom he regarded as friends. Therefore, he must hold Bea as a friend.

"Both fear and freedom keep me from seeking a wife at this particular time in my life," he said. "Being a husband and father comes with great responsibilities, to which, to be blunt, I am not certain I feel equal." His lips curled into a smile. "And then, I do enjoy my freedom. My time is mine to a large extent, as is my income." He shrugged. "It is not perhaps the best of answers, for it certainly does not show me to best advantage, but there it is."

Bea tipped her head and, much to Graeme's annoyance, smiled sweetly at Shelton. "Perhaps it does not show you to good advantage amongst a group of your peers, but to us ladies, it is a very good answer."

Shelton's brows furrowed. "It is?"

Bea nodded. "You view your family as a responsibility not to be taken lightly. You know that your sole claim to your time and money, as well as other freedoms, will need to be abandoned for the wellbeing of a wife and children. That is very commendable, is it not, Grace?"

"Oh, indeed, it is," Grace agreed, her head bobbing up and down vigorously.

"And I suspect, as my mother would say," Bea continued, "when the right person comes along, it will not feel like a loss of freedom but the gaining of a great treasure, and your fear of failure will pale when compared to your fear of losing that lady."

Graeme would gladly give up his freedom rather than lose Bea. His eyes turned to his brother who seemed to be interested in the conversation but not overly affected.

"That is exactly what she would say," Max agreed.

Shelton was quiet for a moment. "I had not considered it in such a light. You are incredibly wise, Miss Tierney. I almost wish I were making you an offer."

"You do not," Bea said with a laugh.

He smiled and shook his head. "No, you are right, but it is not because there is anything lacking in you."

"I hope one day there will be another who agrees," she said softly.

He patted the hand that lay on her lap. "I am certain there will be." His eyes fell once again on Graeme. "Mr. Clayton, what say you?"

"I say Max is next."

Max laughed. "My answer is short. I am not fearful of marriage. I have cared for a mother and sister for some time now, so I do not feel completely unprepared. However, I do enjoy the limited freedom I have and have not met the lady who makes me wish to be parted from that freedom." He turned to Graeme. "Now it is your turn."

Graeme did not like the twinkle in Max's eye. The fellow had been teasing him about courting his sister and being jealous of Shelton, and now that they were speaking about marriage, he was fearful that Max would ask if he wished to marry Bea. How would he answer that? To lie and say he did not wish it might cause Bea to think he did not care for her. However, if he said he did wish to marry her — as he did — and she did not wish to marry him, as she likely did not since she was in love with his brother, their friendship would be broken.

"I need only to find the lady who will accept me," he said.

"You do not fear it?" Grace asked.

Graeme shook his head. "No, I fear loneliness more."

"Are you sure you still need to find the lady?" Shelton asked with a grin. "Surely there is one who has made you think of loneliness?"

Graeme shrugged. "I did not say that I had not found a lady I wish to marry. I said I need to find one who would accept my offer of marriage." He forced his eyes to stay focused on his friend rather than allowing them to shift to Bea.

"You are in love?" Bea asked in surprise.

His eyes met hers as he nodded. "I believe I am." His heart did not know whether to ache or rejoice at the disappointment he read in her expression. Perhaps there was some hope that she could be swayed from loving his brother to loving him.

Chapter 8

THE EVENING AIR SETTLED in, cool and refreshing, as the sun began to dip toward the horizon. Bea once again found herself sitting in the garden while the others wandered along the paths at Stratsbury. Tomorrow morning, Felicity and Grace would be leaving for the Abernathys', and with them, would go Everett and Mr. Shelton — one to attend the house party and the other to his own estate. At the moment, each gentleman had one of her cousins on his arm.

Grace had been undaunted by Mr. Shelton's answers yesterday morning. In fact, it appeared as if she had taken them as a sort of challenge — a call to arms in disabusing the gentleman of his concerns about being ready for marriage and coaxing him to give up his love of the freedom that bachelorhood afforded.

Bea had made it to the middle of the garden before her ankle's protests had overcome her determination to complete the circuit. Graeme had offered to sit with her while the others walked, but after a few moments of persuasion by Bea, he had continued walking and talking with Max.

She smiled as he turned ever so slightly to look back at her. He was very attentive — he had always been so. Being the eldest of the group of boys by one year, he had always made certain she was safe — even if it meant opposing Max. Max had bristled at the idea of anyone thinking he did not care well enough for his sister, but he had also recognized when Graeme was determined and knew that to push him would only result in a fight — one that Max was likely to lose.

Bea leaned against the back of the bench on which she sat sideways with her legs stretched out on the length of the seat. As she rested her head on her hand, she considered the changes that were to occur in the near future. Her familiar little group was about to splinter and shift.

She closed her eyes and allowed herself to feel the disappointment of Everett's being lost to her. She tried to remember what it was about him that had first drawn her interest, but she could not. She had always just preferred his more serious nature. He had spent many hours reading as a boy and been teased mercilessly by Graeme for doing so.

They had that in common. Graeme had always teased her about her love of reading as well.

She shook her head and chuckled. It was not as if Graeme did not read. He did, and he enjoyed the activity to an extent, especially if he could read the piece of literature aloud and in a dramatic fashion. He was more lively than Everett — more like Max in that respect, or her father.

She wrapped a hand around the necklace her father had given her. Even after nine years, she still missed her father dreadfully. Would she ever have a pendant to replace the one he had given her? She sighed. Presently, it seemed unlikely, but the future was unknown. There might yet be someone who would claim her heart as her father had done to her mother's. How she longed for someone to love her in such a fashion. She allowed herself one more bittersweet moment of contemplation about her father before turning her thoughts back to her group of friends.

Everett would be gone. He would marry Felicity — it was obvious that he would –, and then he would take up his living and begin his own family. He would be near — just down the road a mile or two. However, he would have responsibilities that would keep him busy and away from such frequent gatherings as this.

And Graeme? She bit her lip as she considered him. Who would be sitting here with him? Who was it that he loved? She blew out a great breath as the pain of that thought threatened to crush her. She should have known that he would find a lady who would capture his heart, but neither he nor Everett, who had been in town for the season with Graeme, had mentioned anyone in particular. That absence of comment had made the announcement of his being in love quite shocking. If she had been given some indication that her friend was to leave her, she might have been able to face such news without this sadness.

She shook her head and brushed a tear away from the corner of her eye. She was being foolish. He would still be here at Stratsbury. It was not as if he would be truly leaving. His duties were here. However, he would not be so free to meet her in the morning for a ride, and his arm, when strolling in the garden, would always be claimed by someone else.

Change was inevitable. Bea knew this to be true, but the truth of the fact did not make the acceptance of the changes to come any easier.

She, herself, would one day be expected to marry. She knew she could not live forever with Max, no matter how much she wished it. Her brother would eventually take a wife, and there would be new Tierneys to occupy the chairs in the schoolroom and fill the bedrooms at Heathcote.

Max had set money aside for her to have a season, and though she did not relish the idea of going to town, she knew she would have to endure it — for his sake. She was practical enough to know that her greatest chance of securing a good husband would be in those crowded ballrooms of town.

"You promised the rest would be refreshing, but I did not expect you to sleep."

Bea jumped, and her eyes popped open at Max's comment. She had not heard anyone approaching. "Where are the others?" she asked.

"Graeme grew weary of listening to Grace," Max replied with a laugh.

"She never stops speaking!" Graeme muttered. "Shelton can suffer without us bearing witness to it."

"You are a strange friend." Bea swung her legs off the bench and accepted Max's help in rising.

"Shelton would do the same," Graeme said in defense of his actions. "Are you tired? Did we wake you?" Care drenched each word he spoke. It was endearing.

"No, I was not sleeping, although I cannot honestly say I am not a trifle fatigued." She smiled sheepishly at him. "I do not say it to complain or to disparage, but I am looking forward to the quiet that shall be restored to Heathcote on the morrow."

Graeme chuckled. "You are well, then?"

"You looked distraught," Max prodded.

"I was merely pondering life," Bea replied. "We are on the cusp of a new place in our lives. We are children no longer."

Max wrapped an arm around his sister's shoulders. "No, we are not children, but the future does not need to be bleak."

"Oh, it is not; I am sure. Many good things will happen. I am only grieving what has been." She rested her head against Max's shoulder. "I have decided to go to town for the season."

"You have?" Graeme asked in surprise. "But you do not like large crowds."

Bea sighed and nodded. "You know me well." So well. Perhaps better than anyone else. "However, if I am not to be a spinster and a burden to my brother, as well as a disappointment to my mother, I will have to endure the masses."

"Mother will be pleased to hear it," Max said, "but I will not mention it to her until after our cousins have left. I do not wish to listen to their peals of delight and have things twisted in such a fashion that we end up having to take a house with them for three months!"

"I would rather be a spinster," Bea said between giggles.

"I would rather that as well," Max agreed with a shudder. "But it will not happen. You are not the sort of lady to go unloved. Indeed, you have never lacked for a partner at an assembly."

"You are my brother, so you tend to see me in a better light than others."

"No, he has the right of it," Graeme said. "And I have several seasons of ladies with whom to compare you. You shine as brightly as any of them."

"Are you certain you do not wish to court my sister?" Max asked with a smirk.

"This is the thanks I get for supporting your claim?" Graeme cried and appeared, curiously, to be somewhat flustered. "May I not say something flattering without an ulterior motive? Or are you just desperate to be rid of her?"

Max laughed. "I would gladly keep her forever, and I suppose it is not fair to continue to tease you about such things. But you must know, I would be happy to give her to you — not because I wish to be rid of her, but because you have always cared so well for her. And you do suit each other. Your less serious nature balances well with my sister's tendency to ruminate and draw terrible conclusions. Oof," he blew out a breath as Bea's elbow made contact with his side. "You do tend to think of the direst result," he protested.

"I consider the consequences so that I can avoid the direst results," Bea retorted.

"She has a point," Graeme agreed. "She has saved us from disaster more than once."

Max could not deny it, for even though Bea was a good number of years younger than either her brother or Graeme, she had been the one to point out what devastating results some of their boyhood plans might have had.

"I would like to retire to the library for a while," Bea said as they approached the house. "My cousins are departing tomorrow, and I shall once again have time and quiet in which to read."

"I will inform your mother," Graeme said, "and I will come to collect you when she says I must."

"Try to convince her that an hour would be perfect."

"I promise nothing, but I will do my best," he said with a bow before leaving her and Max to find their way to the library.

"You do not need to stay with me," she said as they reached the door. "I shall be well, and I promise not to climb any ladders. The books I wish to read are all within reaching distance with my feet flat on the floor."

"You will not be lonely? You have just spent time sitting alone in the garden. I feel guilty leaving you again."

And he did look as if he felt a great deal of guilt. Her brother liked to have a good time, but he was not one to shirk his responsibilities without feeling the weight of such an offense.

"I asked you to leave me in the garden, and I am asking you to leave me now. You should not feel guilty for doing as I request." She placed her hand on his cheek. "You are an excellent brother." The comment earned her the smile, as well as the solitude, she sought.

She hobbled to the far end of the library to where a group of chairs sat near a window that had been opened to take advantage of the evening air. The book of verses which she wished to read was on the shelf just to the left of the window.

She located it, and another that stood beside it on the shelf, and took them to the chair closest to the fresh air. She lit the lamp on the table as the light from the window was fading, and she would need greater light by which to read.

With a contented sigh, she settled into the chair, tucking herself into the corner of its wing and propping her feet on the footstool that stood in front of it.

Thus she sat, engrossed in the poet's descriptions of the peak district for many minutes. In fact, she had read several poems before her attention was drawn to the window and a rustling and whispering just below it.

She sat quietly, straining to hear what or who might be outside. A giggle floated softly into the room, followed by a low masculine voice, and then silence. As noiselessly as she was able, Bea crept to the window and peeked out to see which of her cousins was in the garden.

She quickly covered her mouth with her hand to catch a gasp as she spotted Felicity and Everett wrapped in what appeared to be a rather passionate embrace. Her heart jumped and skittered to a quicker pace, but it did not ache — not as she expected it should.

Everett was lost to her as she had known he was, but the realization of such a truth did not bring tears to her eyes or a sensation of being crushed as she had feared it would when the inevitable could be denied no longer.

She returned to her book, but her mind would not contemplate the words on the page. It instead wished to consider why her heart had not been more affected. Perhaps it was that she had prepared herself well enough for this moment, or perhaps it was that she did not actually love Everett with the sort of love that drove one to slay dragons and best knights.

There was a bit more rustling outside the window and fading giggles that spoke of Felicity being returned to the house. How the two lovers had been able to escape to the garden, when there were so many eyes to watch them, was puzzling to Bea.

"Everett."

Bea leaned her head toward the window.

"I have been looking for you," Graeme said.

Ah, so Everett and Felicity's absence had not gone unnoticed.

Bea closed her book and stacked it atop the one on her lap. She should move to a place where she would not be tempted to listen to the conversation outside. She placed her books on the table and picked up the lamp, but she did not move as the discourse below her caught her ear.

Graeme apparently knew what his brother had been about in the garden and was scolding him. Her lips curled into a smile. It was rare for Graeme to scold Everett about impropriety. Graeme had often been the receiver of such chiding, but rarely the giver of it.

Bea moved the lamp to a table near another set of chairs and returned to retrieve her books.

"So you never thought of Bea as more than Max's sister?"

Bea paused and waited to hear Everett's reply to Graeme's question. She knew she should not listen, but her curiosity would not allow her to do what was proper until she had heard his response.

"No, never," Everett replied.

Bea's breath caught. It did hurt a bit to know that her love, such that it was, had never been returned and had never had a hope of being requited. But the pain was the just result of doing as she knew she should not. Bea moved quickly away from the window but not fast enough to miss Graeme's next words.

"Neither have I..."

Tears gathered without warning, and a crushing weight threatened to squeeze every last ounce of breath from Bea's chest. This was the pain she had expected to feel when she had seen Everett and Felicity together. This was the pain of love being ripped from her heart. She drew a deep, shuddering breath and blew it out as she clearly realized what her heart had been attempting to tell her over the past few days.

She loved Graeme.

She drew a second breath and released it slowly as she blinked against the tears which accompanied the knowledge that he did not love her in return. She pressed one hand against her aching heart and rubbed her forehead with her other hand, attempting to quiet the throbbing that was beginning behind her eyes. She needed to go home. She needed to climb into her bed and have a good cry. She needed to be away from here and away from him. So, gathering herself as well as she could, she doused the lamp and quietly slipped out of the library, leaving her books and her heart behind.

Chapter 9

As HE WAITED IN Heathcote's drawing room the next afternoon, Graeme flipped through one of the books he had found on a chair in the library at Stratsbury last night when he had gone to collect Bea at the appointed hour. He had been a few moments late in going to the library, since it had taken him longer than expected to find Everett and have a particular, and rather important, discussion with him.

In spite of those delays, Graeme had been surprised to find that Bea had not waited for him, and he was even more surprised when he had discovered she had left her books behind. It was very unlike her and had caused him no little amount of unease.

However, beginning with Shelton cornering him and forcing him to admit his heart was well and truly lost to

Bea, Graeme's day had been unsettling, but not in a truly unpleasant way. That is it was not unpleasantly unsettling until he had found these books where Bea was supposed to have been. Most of the day had been spent in nervous wondering.

First, he had wondered if he would destroy his friendship with Bea if he mentioned his growing attachment to her. Then, after hearing her say she was going to London for the season, and knowing that this must mean she had given up on his brother, he had felt anxiously hopeful when approaching Everett to make certain there would be no danger of damaging their relationship when he made his plans to marry Bea known.

Graeme closed the first book and began paging through the second. He had intended to speak to Bea last night to see if he might have some chance of winning her before she hied off to London in search of another. However, she had been gone before he had gotten the opportunity. All that had been left of her presence had been these books. He snapped the second book shut just as Max entered the drawing room.

"She is resting."

"Is she terribly unwell? I should have never asked her to walk in the garden with me." Graeme ran a hand through his hair. He had been worried about Bea ever since he had returned to the drawing room last night and heard that she had been taken home in a state of ill-health. In fact, he had slept very little last night as a result, and he had not been able to focus on anything today.

Max's head was tipped and his eyes roamed Graeme from head to foot.

"I look a fright." There was no use in denying it. He had not shaven, his hair was rumpled, and his cravat was somewhat askew.

"Indeed, you do. I dare say I have never seen you in such a state outside of when we are in London and have been out excessively late." Max nodded his head toward the door. "Come to my study. Bea will likely be down for tea in a few minutes, and I will ask her if she is feeling up to seeing anyone, although I cannot imagine her refusing to see you even if she is unwell."

"It was not the walk in the garden," Max continued as the two friends walked the short distance down the hall to Max's study.

"It was not?" That was somewhat of a relief.

Max shook his head. "I do not know what caused her to become unwell." He waved to the chairs in front of his desk in an invitation to Graeme to be seated. "All I know is that she came flying out of the library so quickly that I had to catch her to keep her from falling when she knocked into me. I had been on my way to check on her for Mother's sake."

"And you have no idea what was the cause? None at all?"

"No. I questioned her about what might have made her feel so unwell, but unless she took a chill from the open window, I do not know what it was."

Graeme placed the books he carried on the desk. "It was not overly cool last night."

"No, it was not." Max picked up the top book and turned it over in his hands.

"I believe she left those behind in her haste."

Max picked up the second book and turned it over in his hands just as he had with the first book. He gave his friend a curious look and then returned his attention back to the two books on his desk. "I am not sure she will want these. She said there was nothing she wanted at Stratsbury."

Graeme expelled a breath as if he had been punched. Nothing she wanted at Stratsbury. He ran a hand through his hair again. He had known it was a possibility that she would refuse him, but... he had hoped.

"That is just how she said it," Max continued. "While all the while, she rubbed her head and fought tears. It was very odd. I asked if she had not found the book for which she was looking — which we both know is an impossibility because she knows Stratsbury's library so well — but she merely shook her head and repeated that there was nothing at Stratsbury for her." Max tipped his head again, and his brows drew together as he looked at Graeme. "You do not look much better than Bea did last night."

"I did not sleep well. I was worried about Bea."

Max leaned back in his chair. Silence engulfed the room, save for the light tapping of Max's fingers on the edge of his desk and the steady keeping of the time by the clock.

"Are you certain you do not wish to court my sister?" he asked without so much as the slightest twitch of his lips or twinkle in his eye. Though Max was a year younger than Graeme, he appeared to be much older as he slipped from Bea's older brother to her father-figure. "You seem to care for her very much."

He did care for her — more than he thought he could ever care for anyone. He scrubbed his face as he blew out a breath. He was weary, so very weary from not having slept and from worry.

"I want to marry her," he blurted. Rising from his chair, he paced to the window, attempting to ignore Max's startled expression. "I love her."

"You love Bea?"

"I do." With all that was in him, he loved her.

"I know I have teased that you might, but I never imagined it to be true."

"Neither did I." Graeme glanced over his shoulder and smiled sheepishly at Max. "I guess I knew I had always cared for her, but I thought it was only because she was your sister and a friend."

"What changed?"

Graeme shrugged and turned to lean against the window frame. "My brother is an idiot."

Max laughed. "That is not a new revelation to you. You have been saying so for years."

"Yes," Graeme agreed with a grin, "but when he took up with Miss Love and ignored Bea, he sunk to a new level of idiocy." He shook his head. "The more I attempted to get him to realize his stupidity, the more I began to wish he would remain as he was. I did not wish for him to have Bea, but I persisted in my attempts because I wanted Bea to be happy."

A flash of yellow outside the door, which Max had left partially open, caught Graeme's attention, halting his confession.

"Bea," Max called. He held a finger to his lips while looking at Graeme and tipping his head toward the far side of the room.

Graeme nodded his understanding. He would remain silent and hidden until Max wished for him to reveal himself.

Bea must have come to the door, without entering the room, for the door only opened marginally more than it had been open.

"Graeme brought these for you." Max indicated the books on his desk.

"I will collect them later," Bea said softly.

"I think now would be better." Max's tone was demanding, which was unusual for him.

Bea crept into the room, as if she did not wish to claim the books on the desk, but was also unwilling to defy her brother's wishes.

"Graeme had hoped to call on you." Max was intently focused on his sister as if he were attempting to decipher something. "He was concerned about you when you left in such a flutter."

"I do not flutter." Bea folded her arms, and Graeme could just imagine the glare she was giving Max.

Max stood. "Last night you fluttered, but you are correct. It is very unlike you. Are you feeling better now?"

"Yes. Thank you," she replied after a moment's pause. She was hiding something.

"Then, you would not be opposed to entertaining a guest?"

Again, there was a moment's pause before she replied. "Has Mother invited someone to tea?" She shifted uneasily.

Max's lips twitched. Apparently, he also knew that his sister was attempting to play coy. He shifted his attention from Bea to Graeme. "No, I asked you to stay, did I not, Graeme?"

"Indeed, you did."

Her hand flew to her chest and a small squeak escaped her. "Well, then... I suppose I should go see that things are ready," she said without so much as glancing in Graeme's direction and acknowledging his presence.

"No, you should have a seat." Max pointed to one of the chairs in front of his desk before he came around that piece of furniture and perched himself on the edge of it while his sister sat down in front of him.

"Would you like to tell me what it was in particular that made you so unwell last night?" he asked.

Bea shook her head. "No."

Graeme's eyebrows rose. It was a rare occasion when Bea refused outright to do as her brother asked.

Max crossed his arms and smiled. "Am I to understand then, that it is something which you wish for neither me nor Graeme to know?"

Bea said nothing.

"And it happened when you were in the library," he continued as he rubbed his chin.

Bea fidgeted. Max was fairly good at deducing things when his mind was set on discovering what he wanted to know, so Graeme could understand her discomfort.

"You told me that the window was open, and you were sitting near it. However, you do not seem to have caught a chill."

"Your books were not near the window." Graeme took the seat next to her.

She gave him a fleeting glance. "I moved away from the window after –" She snapped her mouth closed.

"After what?" Max asked.

Bea shook her head.

Max's focus did not shift, and the two Tierney siblings sat in silence for a short time just looking at one another until the stalemate ended with a huff from Bea.

"There were people in the garden," she admitted, "and I did not wish to pry into their business by listening to their conversation."

Graeme's heart sank. "Were these people Everett and Miss Love?"

Bea spared him another fleeting glance as she nodded.

"I am sorry they upset you." Perhaps she was more attached to his brother than he had suspected yesterday.

"Why would their being in the garden upset you?" Max asked.

"It was not their being in the garden, but rather what they were doing in the garden," Graeme explained softly. There was no need for Bea to relive what had caused her pain. Therefore, he would not say more than that.

"What were —"

"They did not upset me," Bea interrupted Max's question. "I am not a fool. I knew Everett preferred Felicity, and it is not as if I have never seen anyone kissing before. It happens frequently enough at assemblies."

"Felicity had just returned to the house before you came crashing through the hall. Are you certain they did not upset you?" Max asked.

Graeme watched Bea's expression carefully. She looked exasperated but not as if she were trying to avoid the topic of Felicity and Everett. She must truly not be attached to him.

"I had a headache, my ankle hurt, and there was a tightness in my chest. Can I not have such without it being brought on by emotional distress?"

"You can," Max agreed. "In fact, you have had such on several occasions – often resulting in your being in bed for two days, and Mother threatening to call the apothecary. Neither of those things has happened and…" One eyebrow arched as he gave Bea a pointed look. "You cried."

He held her gaze for a moment longer before pushing off his desk. "I will see if the tea is ready, and Graeme, you can see my sister to the drawing room in ten minutes. There is a matter I wish to discuss with my mother." He gave a nod to Graeme and left before Bea could mount a protest.

She twisted her fingers in her lap.

Graeme could not, for the life of him, figure out why she was so ill-at-ease with him. They had always had a comfortable relationship – until today.

"Thank you for bringing the books." She glanced at him.

"It was my pleasure. I must say that I was surprised to find them, and not you, in the library."

"My apologies. I was not well."

"I had hoped to speak to you about something rather important." He smiled at her when she looked up at him. He would know if he had a chance with her or not before he left this room today. "I was late arriving because I had to speak to my brother first." He ran a hand through his hair and then rubbed both palms on his knees. Breathing was becoming difficult, and his heart was drumming an uncomfortably rapid beat. "I needed to ask him about his intentions regarding Miss Love and his opinion of you."

She closed her eyes. "I know," she whispered. "I heard."

"You heard Everett and me?" Graeme shook his head against the lightness he felt, as his heart seemed to climb into his throat. Had she run away because she heard his confession to his brother about his love for her?

She nodded, daring only to dart a quick look at him. "I did not mean to hear. I was moving away from the window and your voices carried."

Could the world look any bleaker? "I have no hope then?" The words clawed their way out of his mouth, bearing jagged bits of his heart in their grasp.

Bea's brow furrowed as she turned her full attention to him. "Forgive me, but I do not understand. Hope of what?"

Graeme drew a breath and released it. He would survive this – just barely most likely – but he would survive. "Hope of your ever returning my love."

Her eyes grew wide and her mouth opened as if to speak. However, when no sound came out, she closed it again.

Seeing her confusion and finding some hope in it, he continued, "I love you. Is there any hope that you could ever love me in return?"

Bea shook her head, and her mouth opened and closed once more before she found her voice. "You love me?"

The small glimmer of hope he had found moments ago began to burn brighter at the sound of wonder in her words. "Did you not hear me say as much to Everett?"

Slowly, she shook her head from side to side. "You said you had never thought of me as anything other than Max's sister."

Joy split Graeme's face with a smile. He had hope. She might yet accept him. "You did not hear it all."

"I did not?"

"No." A chuckle of pure relief bubbled out. "I asked Everett if he had ever thought of you as more than Max's sister because I needed to know if he would be hurt if I declared myself to you. And he said –"

"He had not," Bea supplied. "And then, you said that you had not either." She blinked at the tears which made her eyes shimmer.

Graeme took her hands in his and slipped off his chair to kneel before her. "I had not considered you beyond that until recently while I was trying to help you win my brother's affections. I kept comparing Miss Love to you and questioning how my brother could prefer someone who was so much..." He searched for the word to describe

Felicity but could not come up with one and so settled on, "Less than you. I envied that you loved Everett."

Her eyes still shimmered, but her lips smiled happily.

"Then, when Shelton came and paid attention to you, I cannot describe how jealous I was. I knew then that I did not want another man to claim you." He shrugged. "But you loved my brother."

She shook her head. "I did not love him. I only thought I did. I was infatuated with his pleasant manners and his serious nature, but I do not believe I ever truly loved him." She looked down at their joined hands. "I knew it the instant I saw him kissing my cousin. My heart should have shattered, but it did not. It pinched with disappointment, but the disappointment did not crush me as I knew it should." She peeked up at him. "It did not crush me as your words did. I love you. Not Everett. Only you."

Elation washed over him. "You love me?"

Bea nodded. "I do."

"Enough to marry me?"

Again, Bea nodded. "Yes."

"You will be mine?"

Bea laughed as she nodded a third time. "Forever," she assured him.

Forever. She was his, and he was hers.

He wanted to sweep her into his arms, but he hesitated. "May I kiss you?" A stolen kiss on the cheek was one thing.

A kiss such as the one for which he longed seemed to require her permission.

Bea did not nod for a fourth time. Nor did she once again tell him yes. His always proper and simply lovely Bea leaned forward and pressed her lips to his before saying with a playful smile, "You shock me with your reserve. I had not thought you capable of such."

He rose from the floor and pulled her to her feet. "I did tell you that I was constitutionally incapable of not being shocking, did I not?"

Her lips were still smiling with amusement in the most beguiling way. "Indeed, you did, Mr. Clayton."

"Graeme," he corrected as he pulled her into his embrace and lowered his head to kiss her.

"My Graeme," she whispered against his lips.

"My beautiful Bea," he replied before claiming her lips with a kiss that was deep and passionate, mingling their souls, declaring his troth, and engraving her on his heart forever.

If you enjoyed this book, be sure to let others know by leaving a review.

Want to know when other Leenie books will be available?
You can always know what's new with my books by joining one of my reader communities
leeniebrown.com/subscribe

On the next page you will find an excerpt of another one of Leenie's books.

His Darling Friend Excerpt

[IT SEEMS ROGER IS going to the Abernathys' house party after all, because his dear friend is there, and it's her birthday. His Darling Friend is book two in the Touches of Austen Collection and gives a small nod to Jane Austen's Emma. Below is how that book begins.]

Chapter 1

Roger Shelton slumped down on the cream-coloured settee in the far corner of the Abernathy's drawing room next to a pretty young lady whom he knew would not bat her lashes at him or smile coyly as all the other eager young women at this house party seemed wont to do. Not that he blamed them, of course. He would make a fine catch if he were ready to be caught.

"Why must we attend these things?" The petite blonde next to him whispered.

"Because neither you nor I are married, and our parents wish to be rid of us," Roger replied.

How often had he heard his mother bemoaning his un-married state to her mother, who would return her own tale of woe about having an unwed daughter? It seemed to be a frequent bent in nearly every conversation when their two families gathered for tea, dinner, or whatever excuse either her mother or his could conjure for themselves to be together.

"Perhaps your mother would like to see someone take over your care, but my father is not anxious to send me packing," his companion retorted.

Roger chuckled. He enjoyed these moments of unfet-tered banter with his friend. She would speak openly to him, for she wanted nothing from him. Not a kiss, not a dance, not a marriage – with her, he was free to be himself. Even if that often led to her scolding him.

"Is that so, Vic? Then why do you suppose your father gave me this." He withdrew a small packet from his pocket and handed it to her. "I was to deliver it to you here with the accompanying message that he trusts your decisions but would like to meet the chap before the vows are read."

With a resounding thump, Victoria Hamilton's right hand connected with Roger's chest, causing him to exhale quickly. She was not one to pull her punches as some chits might. She did not care one jot if Roger thought her less than delicate, and he liked that about her.

"He said nothing of the sort. You are the worst liar – no! I cannot say that. I know you to be a very good liar – but in this, you shall not deceive me."

"It was worth a try," Roger admitted, rubbing the slightly sore spot on his chest where she had hit him.

He had known she would not believe him. Her father was too kind to tease in such a fashion, and he was in no rush to see his darling daughter given away to anyone.

"Your father did give me that package for you. That is the truth. As is the fact that my mother suggested I take a good turn through the ladies of the room looking for more than pleasant curves and a willing smile."

"You are dreadful!"

Roger placed a hand on his heart. "I promise you she said that very thing. Mother is not known for her delicacy when chiding me." In that way, Victoria was a lot like his mother. "There was also something in her diatribe about grandchildren before she turned her toes up." He shot a devilish grin at his friend.

"Do not say it," Victoria hissed.

It amused him how her expression was appropriately appalled at the mere thought of what he was about to say. She did know him well. Of course, her expression would not prevent him from continuing.

"Mother was not pleased when I suggested that producing children did not require a marriage license."

"You did not!" Victoria shook her head. "Of course, you did. I can nearly hear you saying it."

"I am wounded."

"By the truth?"

"No, by the thought that you think I would –" A severe glare stopped his words.

"Are you or are you not, Roger Shelton, the charmer of ladies, the stealer of kisses, the seeker of pleasure?"

He could not refute her statement, so he did not. He simply sat quietly and waited for her to continue.

"None of that embarrasses you as it should," she muttered. "Did you get your hunter?"

Apparently, the discussion of his ill behaviour was at an end.

He nodded and extended his feet out in front of him, crossing them at the ankles and making himself very comfortable. "Clayton helped me."

"Mr. Clayton?" she asked with a smile that caused him to raise a brow in question. "He is pleasant," she retorted with a huff. "Naught else."

"That is good to know since I do believe he is getting married. At least he seemed on the point of proposing when I left Stratsbury Park, and I dare say the lady was only waiting for him to ask. She'll accept him, happily."

"Indeed?" Her tone was filled with delight.

"Thanks to my assistance."

Victoria blinked, and her mouth dropped open for a moment. "I beg your pardon?" she asked incredulously.

Was it so impossible to believe that he would help a friend in such a way? He supposed it likely was. He was not known as the sort of gentleman who looked for ways to be snared. But then, he was setting the parson's trap for his friend and not himself, so it really should be more believable.

"I may have pointed out to Clayton how he and his neighbour Miss Tierney would suit each other quite well."

"You?" There was not a single ounce of belief in her tone. "You helped a fellow charmer make a match?"

Ah, that was why she was so disbelieving. It was not just any gent he had helped. Graeme Clayton was nearly as much a rogue as he himself was. Roger shrugged and puffed out his chest a bit. "I have always been very good at reading people."

She shook her head.

Why did she have such a difficult time believing that he could do anything good?

"I assure you I am. How else have I remained a bachelor for so long when there are so many who would trip over each other to be my bride." He winked at her, and she rolled her eyes, just as he knew she would.

"I am certain I could find a match within the assembled hopefuls. Not for myself," he clarified. "I am not in any hurry to be married, but several gents seem eager and, yourself excepted, there is not a lady here who is not hoping to snare a husband."

"I am not the only lady who does not feel a need to rush to the altar," Victoria retorted as if he had affronted her most grievously, but there was a small curl of her lips that told him she was not entirely put out with him.

He leaned toward her. "Marrying at three and twenty would not be rushing," he muttered near her ear.

"Oh, good heavens, you have been talking to my mother, have you not?"

Roger nodded. "Why do you not marry?"

"Why should I?"

"Do you really wish to live with your brother and his wife?"

Victoria expelled a great sigh but said nothing. Roger knew very well that Victoria did not like the new Mrs. Hamilton and had been quite delighted to hear that her brother and his new wife would be spending a great deal of time in town or at a rented cottage near the sea when the weather got too warm to abide London.

"Why do you not marry?" she asked instead of answering his question.

"I do not marry for quite noble reasons, or so Miss Tierney says."

The brow over her left eye rose skeptically. "And what pray tell are your noble reasons?"

Roger folded his arms and looked at her — his dear friend who did not believe there was a noble bone in his body. "Do you not think me capable of being honourable?"

Her lips pursed, and her brow furrowed. "It is not that you are incapable of such," she said after a full minute of silence. "You know that I have always told you how honourable you could be. You have the potential to be a very fine gentleman who is sought after for more than his looks and a bit of fun."

Her cheeks coloured slightly as she said those last words. Impropriety of the sexual nature always made Victoria blush when she referenced it. She was as proper as he was improper. She might not agree with all of society's strictures, but her behavior was always impeccable. She assured him that it was possible to both disagree and still adhere to the rules. He was not certain he believed her.

"If you think me capable of being honourable, then why do you question so vehemently as to whether or not my reasons are noble?"

She expelled an exasperated huff. "Because I see little evidence of your nobility when it comes to the fairer sex." The blush on her cheeks deepened a shade. "And I did not question you vehemently. I questioned. That is all."

Roger's lips tipped up on one side. "I will only tell you my reasons after you have told me your reasons for not marrying."

Her eyes grew wide, and she shook her head. "I cannot."

"Cannot or will not?"

"Will not."

That answer stopped Roger from any further prodding. They had not had any secrets – or at least not many secrets – ever. They had shared nearly everything with one another growing up, and it bothered him that she would choose now to decide she would keep something so interesting from him.

"I would not tease you," he offered.

"I know you would not, but..." She sighed and shook her head. "I would feel too foolish."

She did not trust him. She said she thought him capable of nobility, and yet, she did not actually trust him. It stung as much as if she had slapped him. He drew a breath and released it.

"Very well," he said, "then, I shall not tell you mine. You may write to Miss Tierney to discover them if you wish, but I shall not tell you."

"I have hurt you," she said softly as she placed a hand on his still folded arms.

Feeling very much like a petulant child, he merely shrugged and changed the subject – somewhat.

"Who shall we see matched?" He would prove to her in some way that he was capable of thinking about marriage in a serious fashion.

"I really could not say," she replied. Her brow was furrowed. "Are you well? I did not mean to – "

"Perfectly," he cut off her apology. He did not wish to hear it at present. "I am perfectly well."

He was not. His closest friend in all the world had just told him in so many words that she did not trust him. However, he was not about to admit to it.

"I say we spend a day considering who might complement whom at this gathering, and then I shall begin." He leaned close to her and nudged her shoulder with his. "If you would be so kind, I should rather appreciate it if you would attempt to discover which sort of gentleman we might match with Miss Grace Love."

"Why?"

There was that skepticism again.

"She knows my reasons for not wishing to marry since we played a little game when I was visiting Clayton, and rather than heeding the fact that I have no desire to marry, she has taken it upon herself to follow me around and attempt to prove my reasons are not insurmountable." He lowered his voice. "Frankly, I do not trust her. She is very marriage minded and only seventeen." He shuddered.

"Far too young to be attached to an old man such as yourself?"

"Far too flighty. And I am not old. Might I remind you that you are only four years younger than me?"

"Younger is the important word," Victoria said with a laugh that always lifted his spirits — even when he was put out with her. "I shall see what I can learn about Miss Love."

"Thank you." Roger pulled a second small package from his pocket and after rising handed it to her.

"What is this?" She turned the item over in her hands.

He smiled. "Did you really think, my darling friend, that I would not remember your birthday as I always have?" He winked and then giving her a bow, left her so that she could open his gift in private.

Acknowledgements

THERE ARE MANY WHO have had a part in the creation of this story. Some have read and commented on it. Some have proofread for grammatical errors and plot holes. Others have not even read the story (and a few, I know, will never read it), but their encouragement and belief in my ability, as well as their patience when I became cranky or when supper was late or the groceries ran low, was invaluable.

And so, I would like to say thank you to Zoe, Rose, Betty, Kristine, Ben, and Kyle. I feel blessed through your help, support, and understanding.

I have not listed my dear husband in the above group because, to me, he deserves his own special thank you, for without his somewhat pushy insistence that I start sharing my writing, none of my writing goals and dreams would have been met.

More Books by Leenie

You can find all of Leenie's books at this link
bit.ly/LeenieBBooks
where you can explore the collections below

Dash of Darcy and Companions Collection
Marrying Elizabeth Series
Sweet Possibilities and Sweet Extras
Willow Hall Romances
The Choices Series
Darcy Family Holidays
Darcy and... An Austen-Inspired Collection
Teatime Tales (Sweet Austen-inspired Novelettes)

Other Pens

Touches of Austen

Nature's Fury and Delights (Sweet Regency Novelettes)

You can also find free-to-listen-to books on YouTube
at youtube.com/@leeniebbooks

About Leenie

Leenie Brown has always been a girl with an active imagination, which, while growing up, was both an asset, providing many hours of fun as she played out stories, and a liability, when her older sister and aunt would tell her frightening tales. At one time, they had her convinced Dracula lived in the trunk at the end of the bed she slept in when visiting her grandparents!

Although it has been years since she cowered in her bed in her grandparents' basement, she still has an imagination which occasionally runs away with her, and she feeds it now as she did then — by reading!

Her heroes, when growing up, were authors, and the worlds they painted with words were (and still are) her favourite playgrounds! Now, as an adult, she spends much of her time in the Regency world, playing with the characters from her favourite Jane Austen novels and those of her own creation.

When she is not traipsing down a trail in an attempt to keep up with her imagination, Leenie resides in the beautiful province of Nova Scotia with her two sons and her very own Mr. Brown (a wonderful mix of all the best of Darcy, Bingley, and Edmund with a healthy dose of the teasing Mr. Tilney and just a dash of the scolding Mr. Knightley).

Connect with Leenie in one of her reader communities or on social media. Find links to all of those on her website at bit.ly/connect-with-leenie